Trapped.

They stood very close together, their eyes scanning the attic in dread, their breath coming in short, anxious gasps.

"This is unreal," Daisy said, staring down at Lynne. "How could someone have brought her into the house and up here without any of us hearing or seeing him? Up all those stairs . . ."

"Oh, no," Toni whispered, her hands clutching the edge of the trunk, "he's *in* here! He's in the house!" Words spilled out of her mouth as panic overtook her. "He's not outside, he's in *here* somewhere, with us . . ."

Terrifying thrillers by Diane Hoh:

Funhouse
The Accident
The Invitation
The Train
The Fever

NIGHTMARE HALL

Captives

DIANE HOH

SCHOLASTIC INC.
New York Toronto London Auckland Sydney

No part of this publication may be reproduced in whole or in part, or stored in a retrieval system, or transmitted in any form or by any means, electronic, mechanical, photocopying, recording, or otherwise, without written permission of the publisher. For information regarding permission, write to Scholastic Inc., 555 Broadway, New York, NY 10012.

ISBN 0-590-25081-7

12 11 10 9 8 7 6 5 4 3 2 1   5 6 7 8 9/9 0/0

Printed in the U.S.A.   01

First Scholastic printing, July 1995

NIGHTMARE HALL

Captives

Prologue

He just keeps talking and talking and talking. His mouth flaps open and shut, open and shut, like that dumb goldfish I had when I was eight instead of the puppy I really wanted. Every time I think he's finally going to shut up and let me talk, he opens his mouth again.

He never lets me talk. Loves the sound of his own voice too much. But he's getting paid to listen, isn't he? Isn't that what a shrink is supposed to do?

"Let me talk!" I scream at him, and he looks up at me like I've lost my mind.

Oh, that's funny. That's really funny. Of course I've lost my mind, or I wouldn't be in this stupid office in the first place with the eminent Dr. Milton Leo, would I?

"Now, now," he says, "there's no need to shout." He lays aside his notebook, sits up straighter in his chair, and I can see something

in his eyes that I've never seen before.

Fear.

He's afraid of me! What a rush! Mr.-I-Am-In-Control-Here-At-All-Times is not so cool now, is he? All because of one tiny little shout.

I like the effect so much, I decide to shout some more. And once I start, I can't stop. I shout and I shout. I tell him he's a stupid jerk who doesn't know the first thing about psychiatry, that he's the one who needs the shrink, not me. I shout that if he tells me one more time I have to take responsibility for my own actions, I'm going to hit him with that big gold lamp on the table beside his left elbow.

And then that's what I do.

I don't mean to. It's not something I think about ahead of time. But the lamp is sitting right there beside him and it looks so heavy and so solid and I can't resist it.

He was supposed to help me, and he didn't.

I think the reason he doesn't move out of the way in time is he can't believe it's happening. Not to him. That's what I see in his face as I lunge for the lamp, grab it off the table, and bring it down hard on the left side of his head. I see astonishment in those dark, cold eyes behind the glasses. Not me, he's thinking.

So much blood. I expected ice-water to flow

from that coldhearted creep, but it's blood, all right.

I feel bad for Tanner. He's her father, after all. I guess they didn't get along that great, but still . . . Tanner was always nice to me.

But, he made *me* do it! Sitting there so smug, so pompous, passing judgment on me. Shrinks aren't supposed to pass judgment. Then he had to go and bring up that nasty business two years ago. That wasn't my fault, either, but he made it sound like it was.

I need to think, but my head aches really bad.

He never even screamed. I know he told people that I wasn't violent. I saw one of the reports he signed. I'll bet he was sorry he ever wrote that when he saw that lamp coming at him.

Think, think . . .

This is the worst. I can't hide this. No way. His secretary has gone home. She never saw me come in. And I didn't have an appointment, just dropped in on the off chance that he'd see me, so no one knows I was here except him and me. And neither one of us is going to tell.

But the police will check out his patients and they'll find out about two years ago and they'll come looking for me. They'll put me away again.

I can't go back to that place. I won't.

Don't panic, panic is the worst thing. It makes the headaches unbearable.

Think, think . . .

There has to be a way.

They're not taking me back there. I'll do anything to stay out of that place.

Anything.

The first thing is, to get out of here. But how far can I go in this storm? The roads might be washed out.

I have to find a place to hide.

Somewhere where no one would think to look for me . . .

I think I know just the place . . .

Chapter 1

The rain came at them out of the darkness at a wind-blown slant, silvery sheets of it slapping against the car. The windshield wipers made a steady, annoying, whoosh-whoosh sound as they worked frantically to do their job.

"We should have left Briscoe this afternoon instead of waiting until after supper," Lynne Grossman told the three passengers in her new silver Toyota Camry. The car had been an unabashed bribe in return for Lynne's grudging participation in a two-week July math refresher course at Salem University in preparation for freshman year beginning in September. The trip to the university was her first long drive in the new car. "This weather stinks! It's raining so hard, I can't see three feet in front of the car, and the defogger isn't working."

"We couldn't leave earlier," Daisy Rivers

said. She was occupying the passenger's seat. Her left hand repeatedly dove into a bag of cheese snacks, but she chewed and swallowed before she spoke. "I was working, remember? Unlike you, my parents didn't buy me a brand-new car, and they're not going to. If I want one, I have to earn the money myself. My boss said if I worked up until the very last minute, he'd hold my job for me while I'm at Salem for two weeks. I need that job when I get back, Lynnie."

"I know." Lynne swiped at the misted windshield with one hand. "I didn't mean it was your fault, Daisy. Quit being so hyper." She said it calmly, matter-of-factly, as she said almost everything. The fact that she now owned a car wasn't the only difference between her and Daisy. Lynne was tall and athletic, with smooth, silky, very short, dark hair. She was efficient and even-tempered, except when her unexplained ability to grasp mathematical concepts made her crazy.

Daisy was tall, too, but there the similarities ended. Daisy Rivers was thin and blonde and deceptively fragile-looking, with small bones and a heart-shaped face. But she was anything but fragile, and anything but calm. She was energetic and high-powered. It was hard for her to sit still for more than a few minutes.

When she wasn't sitting in a car, she was in a state of perpetual motion, impatient and always prodding others to move at her pace. Few did.

Being a friend of Lynne's was easy. Being a friend of Daisy's was not. But Daisy was loyal to the core and fiercely protective of her friends, and most people felt that made it worthwhile.

Daisy was no more interested in taking the summer math session than she was in hopping a shuttle to the moon, but her acceptance at Salem was conditional . . . take the course and pass it or we won't take *you*. No choice. She would much rather have left Briscoe for New York City the day after her high school graduation and make her mark out in the world. No more classes, no more homework, no more papers to write, and no more math. That would have been her first choice.

But Daisy Rivers had been poor all of her life. She was smart enough to know that without some formal training, the dresses, skirts, blouses, and pants and jackets that she designed in a huge sketch pad, would never become reality. Without Salem University, she would *stay* poor, and that wasn't what she wanted.

College might be a drag, but it was the only

way to get to where she wanted to be.

"We've already been driving for almost three hours," Toni Davinci complained from the back seat. "If we don't get out of this car soon, my body is going to stay permanently frozen in this position."

"I second the motion," Molloy Book agreed. She was slouched down beside Toni, her long legs in black leggings stretched out in front of her, her feet in black flats propped up on the armrest between Lynne and Daisy. "I hate this weather! It gives me the creeps. But right now I'd take my chances out there if it'd get me out of this back seat."

Lynne leaned forward, peering through the misted windshield. "Oh, no!" she cried in a voice that made both Toni and Molloy sit upright. Lynne pointed. "A detour sign! Oh, I don't believe this. I don't know my way around this area well enough to take a detour."

The other three stared through watery windows at the huge orange sign lit by a hanging lantern. DETOUR, ROAD FLOODED.

"There will be other signs, pointing the way," Molloy said. "They'll show us how to get back on the highway."

Lynne groaned. "This is all I need! A stupid detour! As if bad weather and a defective defroster aren't enough."

"Calm down," Daisy said. "We have to be almost there. Let's just go. Anyway, a detour is better than driving on a flooded road, right? I can't swim."

"Neither can I," Toni echoed from the back seat. "What's the detour road look like? It's not one of those awful dirt roads, is it? It'll be a sea of mud after all this rain."

"How should I know?" Lynne snapped. "I told you, I can't see a thing." But she steered the car off the highway and onto the side road. Without the illumination of highway pole lights, she drove more slowly and, after a few minutes, said in dismay. "It *is* a dirt road! And Toni was right, it's all mud. I can feel the tires sliding."

Molloy slid back down in the back seat. This trip was supposed to be a lark. Of the four of them, only she had been enthusiastic about attending the special math session at Salem. But her enthusiasm had more to do with the fact that her boyfriend Ernie Dodd was already on campus. He was attending full summer school in an effort to get a jump-start on his college education.

She couldn't wait to see Ernie. He'd been gone two weeks already and it seemed like two years. They had talked on the phone every night, while her parents sat in the living room pretending to watch television. They weren't. They were straining to hear every word of her conversation, their mouths pursed in disapproval. Not that they had anything against Ernie personally. How could anyone not like Ernie?

But the Dodds, all eight of them, lived on the "wrong side of town." Molloy's family lived on the "right side." Ernie's father worked in a factory. Molloy's parents owned their own small but successful dry-cleaning shop. A Dodd wasn't exactly what they had in mind for their daughter. What they had in mind was a handsome, cultured, premed or prelaw student driving an expensive car, whose family lived on the *right* side of town.

Ernie Dodd hoped to be a writer, a profession Molloy's parents considered financially precarious. His car was an ancient pickup truck with its back window missing, and he honked the horn at the curb when he came to pick her up, instead of coming up to the house and knocking. Not that she blamed him. Her parents treated people who came to the house to sell magazines or vacuum cleaners better than they treated Ernie.

He was absolutely, positively, not what they wanted for her.

But Ernie Dodd, tall, awkward, and always,

always badly in need of a decent haircut, was *exactly* what she wanted for herself. Ernie was funny and sweet and thoughtful and never, ever apologized for who he was or where he lived, which Molloy would have hated.

But because she had insisted on attending the same college as Ernie, her parents had refused to help her so she was going to have to work her way through, with the help of several small scholarships. Other people did it. She could do it, too, and would, if it meant being with Ernie.

Her parents would come around one day. Ernie was hard to resist.

They had been on the dirt road for fifteen minutes, the rain hammering down on the car roof, when Lynne said, "I have not one clue where we are. All I know is, we've been driving for hours. We should have reached Salem by now. Maybe we're lost."

"We're not lost," Daisy scoffed. "How could we be lost?"

"Well, where are all those other detour signs you mentioned, Molloy? I haven't seen a single one."

"We just haven't got to them yet," Molloy replied with less confidence than she felt. "So that means we're right on course. When we're supposed to turn, there will be a sign telling us to turn."

"Unless the wind blew it down," Toni said. She clutched her violin case tightly. It contained her most precious possession, the violin she had treasured since she was six years old and had lovingly nicknamed Arturo. She often joked that if a thief ever broke into her house, he'd have to kill her to get the musical instrument away from her. She was only half-joking.

Toni was only taking the math course at Salem because her friends were. She understood mathematics as well as she understood music. They seemed similar to her, and neither had ever given her a problem. But she was anxious to get to college. Attending summer school meant that in August, when they all entered for real, Salem wouldn't feel so new and strange. She hated that feeling . . . being someplace new, not feeling like she belonged.

It was hard to imagine any of her friends ever feeling like they didn't belong. Molloy had been president or vice-president of practically everything in high school, and Daisy was always surrounded by a group of people. It was hard, too, to imagine either of them afraid.

I'm afraid *now*, Toni thought, her hands seeking comfort from the violin case. Lynne isn't that familiar with this car yet, the road is a sea of mud, we can't see out of the windows, and I haven't noticed the lights of a single house since we got on this road.

"Maybe we should turn around and go back," Toni said hesitantly. "We could find a gas station on the highway and ask for directions."

"That wouldn't take away the detour," Lynne pointed out sensibly. "We'd still have to go this way." Her head turned from side to side. "Anybody see any lights?"

No one did.

"When they build a road," Lynne said angrily, "why can't they build it straight? It's making me crazy, one curve after another, and I can't *see* them until I'm right on top of them."

"They don't make them straight," Daisy said, "because sometimes there's a *town* in the way, Lynne. What do you want them to do, mow down everything in their path just so you won't have to turn a corner?"

Lynne shot her a disdainful glance.

Taking her eyes off an unfamiliar road for even a second in such bad weather conditions spelled disaster. The car swerved on the muddy surface and the rear wheels slid to the right.

Lynne gripped the steering wheel and fought to straighten the car. But in her panic, she overcorrected.

The car skidded, slid, then the wheels took hold and the car shot across the road and dove, nose down, into a shallow ditch overflowing with rainwater.

The engine made a soft, sighing sound as if to say, "Now look what you've done!" and died.

Chapter 2

It's a good thing I saw their headlights coming down on the back road and came out to check. If I hadn't been looking out the upstairs window just then, I'd have never known anyone was out here. I suppose they saw my light, too. That's why they're headed this way. They saw my light and now they think there's someone up here to save them. That's a laugh.

Shouldn't have had my light on. But I was on the back side of the house and didn't expect anyone to see it. There's nothing out there but woods.

What are they doing out in this weather, anyway? Lost, I suppose. That damn detour. If it weren't for that, I'd be long gone, myself.

Things were going to be okay. They were. No one knew where I was. And who would have thought to look for me here? I could have stayed until the roads were clear, and then split. But now, I've got unexpected visitors. They could ruin everything for me.

Any second now, they'll be at the top of the hill, they'll see the house, they'll want to come in and get warm and dry.

Well, I'm sorry, little Missies, I was here first. Squatters' rights. In pioneer times, people were killed for infringing on squatters' rights.

Now there's a thought.

I wonder if it's easier the second time?

Maybe I won't have to use such drastic measures. I could try and scare them off first. Since they don't know I'm out here. And since they probably aren't expecting to meet anyone out here in the middle of the woods on a night like this. Scaring them could send them racing back down that hill.

If scaring them doesn't work, well, it's all their fault. They've spoiled everything. So if more drastic measures are called for, they have only themselves to blame. Not me. It's not my fault.

Why are people always getting in my way? Why can't they leave me alone?

Before the night is over they'll wish they had.

Chapter 3

Ernie Dodd sat in front of the computer in his small, cluttered room in Devereaux Hall on the campus of Salem University, his fingers poised but unmoving on the keyboard. A large, framed photo of Molloy sat at his elbow at an angle that made it look as if she were smiling directly at him. Shaggy, dark brown hair touched the shoulders of his denim jacket as he tilted his head to listen to the words of the campus radio announcer who had interrupted Ernie's train of thought by beginning his announcement with the phrase, "Special bulletin."

Something about the weather, Ernie guessed.

Instead, as Ernie listened attentively, he heard, *"This news just in. University officials have announced that the body of Dr. Milton Leo, a member of the Salem faculty and a practicing psychologist, has been discovered in his campus office. According to police, Dr. Leo's death was caused by repeated blows to the head with a blunt object. There was no forced entry of the premises, and the whereabouts of the assailant at this time are unknown.*

"Police report there is a list of suspects who will be questioned immediately. Those names have not been released.

"Dr. Leo's only survivor is a daughter, Tanner Melissa Leo, a sophomore at the university.

"This station will provide more details on the incident as they arrive."

Then, as abruptly as it had ended, music began again.

Murdered? Dr. Leo had been murdered?

Ernie, his hands still poised on the keyboard, felt sorry for Tanner, who had only recently reached some kind of peace with her father. Because of a divorce when she was very young, she hadn't known him when she was growing up and had only come to Salem to live with him so she could go to college. They'd had some rough moments; everyone knew that Dr. Leo was a cold fish. Completely the opposite of Tanner. But was that reason enough to bash in the guy's skull?

Ernie's eyes moved to Molloy's photograph.

He thought of Molloy finally making it to Salem even though her parents didn't approve.

"They're never going to like me," he told the photo matter-of-factly. "We both know that, Molloy. And it's going to make for a pile of problems somewhere down the road."

Didn't matter. Well, it mattered, but they'd handle it. He wasn't giving up Molloy. He'd put up with a lot of garbage in his life because he knew that was just the way things were.

But then, on a really rotten, cold, rainy day in October of his junior year of high school, he'd met Molloy Book.

At Christmastime of that year, Molloy had said, although he hadn't asked how she felt about him because he hadn't had the nerve, "I really like you a lot, Ernie Dodd. And I think I'm always going to." And all he'd given her, all he could afford to give her, was a stupid tape he'd made of her favorite Christmas song, and his football sweater. She didn't seem to care that it wasn't a cashmere sweater or expensive jewelry.

He wasn't giving up Molloy. Not for anything.

Thinking about her sent his eyes to the watch on his wrist. The placement of its hands jolted him upright. Eight-thirty! Eight-thirty? That couldn't be right. If it was really eight-thirty, Molloy would be here by now. She had said six, and she was never late. Six o'clock, she'd said. Two-and-a-half hours ago?

Ernie got up and strode to the window, tried to look out. He saw nothing but a slick veneer of rain sliding down the glass.

Maybe that was why Molloy was late. Lynne was driving a car she'd hardly driven at all and with the roads so bad, they'd probably decided to take their time. Hadn't Banion said something earlier on the radio about the highway between school and Twin Falls being flooded? Closed down temporarily? Lynne would have had to come that way from Briscoe. So maybe they'd stopped somewhere. That would have been smart. Waiting it out, until the rain let up.

Ernie went to the phone in the hall to check the time. His watch could be wrong. "The time is now eight-thirty-two p.m., Daylight Savings Time," a smooth voice assured him.

He should have been paying attention, instead of getting so totally lost in his writing. It was a short story for his comp class, due Monday, and it was almost done. He hadn't realized how much time had passed since he first sat down in front of the word processor.

"Aren't you sick and tired of being poor?" his mother had said when he told her he wanted to become a writer. But his father, the person Ernie had expected to really be disappointed that he wasn't shooting for lawyer or doctor or scientist, had said, "If that's what you want, son, go for it. I can't help you out much, you know that, but if you want it bad enough, you'll get it yourself."

And although Molloy's father had said scornfully, "A writer? Aren't you going to get a real job?," Molloy herself had said, "Great! Reading is one of my favorite things and now I won't have to buy the books, you can just write some for me." As if she didn't have the slightest doubt that if he wanted to be a writer, he would be.

But he wondered how she'd feel if he confessed that he hadn't even known she was two and a half hours late because he'd been busy writing.

I should do something, he told himself, beginning to pace back and forth in the small room. But what?

Call Molloy's house, see if she'd left when she said she was going to? If the weather was as bad in Briscoe as it was here, maybe they'd postponed their trip until tomorrow.

No. She would have called him. She knew how he hated calling her house. She wouldn't make him do that if she could help it. If they'd started out and hadn't been able to get through or had decided to wait it out somewhere, she'd have called.

Unless the telephone lines were down where she was. A distinct possibility.

Ernie hurried out into the hall again and lifted the receiver off the wall phone. It was still working, although there was a lot of static.

Ernie replaced the receiver and went back into his room. Just because the phones on campus were working, that didn't mean all the phones in the area were.

He tried to relax, and couldn't. The bad news about Dr. Leo had unsettled him, made his skin crawl. Bad things happened. Even to important people like Dr. Leo. He'd made someone mad and that someone had killed him.

So bad things could happen to Ernie Dodd, too. Already had, more than once. But the very worst thing that he could think of was something bad happening to Molloy Crandall Book. That, he couldn't deal with. No way.

She was probably fine.

Of course, she was fine.

She *had* to be.

Chapter 4

"What *was* that?" Lynne whispered to the three girls flanking her. They stood as still as statues on the mud-slicked slope, listening to see if the rustling in the woods above them came again. They had been glad to leave the ditched car, but they hadn't expected the woods to be so dark.

"Maybe it's someone looking for us," Tony said, her eyes searching the crest of the hill.

"They wouldn't be looking *here*," Daisy said. "Why would they be looking for us in the woods? We're supposed to be on the highway!"

"Maybe someone found the car in the ditch, and figured out that we hiked up the hill," Molloy suggested. "Should we call out or something?"

"No." Lynn waved the flashlight around, but the beam, steadily growing dimmer, revealed only dripping trees and bushes. "Not yet. Let's just listen for a minute. It's probably a raccoon or a squirrel."

"It's just so *dark*," Toni said, her voice quavering slightly. "They don't have bears around here, do they?"

Even Lynne blinked. "Bears?" She waved the flashlight more aggressively, playing it in a circle around them. She had just completed the circle when the pale yellow beam blinked out.

Toni gasped, and Daisy said, "Oh, great. I don't suppose anyone happens to be carrying extra flashlight batteries, do they?"

This time, the sound, still above them, was louder. They could hear it clearly over the rain beating down upon the trees and bushes and leaf-covered ground.

Someone or some*thing* was up there.

"That did not sound like a raccoon," Molloy whispered, one hand reaching out to clutch the sleeve of Daisy's windbreaker. "And if it was someone looking for us, they'd be calling out to see if we were in here."

"Let's go back down," Tony said, her words rushing together with urgency. "Come on, it'll be easier going downhill. We'll go back to the car and wait there for someone to find us."

"I'm too tired to turn around now." Lynne shook the flashlight vigorously, but it refused to come back to life. "Besides, that road is probably an ocean by now. And do you really want to tackle that creek again? I don't. We're almost to the top, and there's a house up there. I can see it. A nice, warm, cozy house, with a telephone. Come on, guys, don't wimp out on me now. There are four of us and we don't even know what's making that noise. It *could* be a raccoon. A big one."

"I'm with Lynne," Molloy said. "I am soaked to the bone, I'm cold, my legs feel like rubber from all this climbing, and I can't face that creek again. Come on, girls, we are women, hear us roar. Whatever that is up there, we can deal with it, right?"

"Absolutely right," Daisy said, turning to face the top of the hill.

"Well, I'm not going back down by myself," Toni said grudgingly. "If you're all going up, I'm coming, too. But could we please stay very close together, now that we don't have any light at all?"

They had all turned toward the top of the hill and joined hands, when they heard a rumbling sound above them. It sounded a little like a large truck moving across the ground.

"What . . . ?" Lynne began, but before she could finish the thought, the deep grumble became an ominous thundering, and the earth seemed to shake beneath their feet.

The boulder came at them from above, shooting out of the thick, dark underbrush like a cannonball, aiming straight at the group holding hands on the muddy, slippery slope.

Chapter 5

The huge boulder thundered down the hill toward them, spraying mud and leaves in its path. Too paralyzed with fear to move, the four girls, still clutching hands and stricken mute with shock, formed a petrified human chain directly in its path.

It was Molloy who screamed, "Move out of the way!"

The sound of her voice spurred them to action. Hands tore free of other hands, bodies flew to the left and to the right, voices cried out in pain as a leg slammed into a fallen log, an elbow cracked against a stone on the ground.

The boulder, which Daisy would describe later with her usual hyperbole as being "the size of a small house," thundered on down the hill, past them, landing, finally, in the creek far below them with a splash that resounded through the woods.

Molloy, weak with relief, lay sprawled on the spongy ground, her head against the rough bark of a fallen tree. She could already feel a lump beginning to rise on the back of her skull. But a lump was nothing in comparison to being squashed flatter than a pancake by a giant rock.

Lynne, holding her left elbow, was lying right beside Molloy. Her face was twisted in pain. "I think it might be broken," she told Molloy.

Molloy helped her up and checked the elbow, as Daisy and Toni, brushing wet dirt and leaves from their clothing, joined them. Toni was holding the flashlight. It was dim, but it was on. Toni was shaking so violently, it swung back and forth like a lantern sending a signal in Morse code. The left side of her face was an angry red. "Rock," she whispered. "Hurts."

Lynne's elbow wasn't broken, after all. She could move the arm back and forth, and when she spotted the baseball bat lying on the ground, she bent to scoop it up, gripping it firmly around the neck, proving that the arm was no more than bruised. She had decided in the car to bring the bat along for protection.

Daisy was intact, although she was thoroughly soaked and covered in mud. "Of course I landed right in the middle of one of those torrents of water gushing down the hill," she said shakily. "But I figure that's better than landing underneath that boulder, right?" Her thin, heart-shaped face, yellow in the flashlight's glow, looked bleak.

"The ground must have given way up there," Lynne said, picking wet leaves from her jeans. "Like during those mudslides in California. If Molloy hadn't screamed, we'd all be leaf mold now."

"How do we know there aren't more boulders up there?" Toni asked, her eyes nervously scanning the top of the hill. "I told you we should have gone back down to the car."

"Oh, right." Daisy bent, twig in hand, to scrape a thick layer of mud from her sneakers. "That way, we just would have been mowed down from behind. When they put us in our coffins, we'd have these weird expressions of total surprise on our faces, as if we were saying, 'Whoa! What was *that*?' "

"Daisy, stop talking about coffins," Lynne commanded. "Nobody died. Nobody's even hurt. And what are the odds that a second boulder is going to break loose of its moorings and come charging down the hill toward us? Probably nonexistent." Rain dripped from her hair, her eyebrows, her nose, and her chin. Her pink cotton T-shirt was plastered to her body like a second skin. "Come on! It's not that much farther."

* * *

"See? What did I tell you?" Lynne cried triumphantly as they came over the rise and found themselves in a clearing occupied by three buildings. There were no lights in any of the windows, but their eyes had become accustomed to the darkness. With the help of the flashlight, they could see on the left side of the clearing a square, squat barn or shed, and on the right, a two-story garage with a set of narrow outside steps leading upward to a door. In the center of the clearing at the top of the hill stood a huge, four-story, old brick building with a small enclosed back porch and a metal fire escape clinging to a side wall. The brick looked almost black, and was nearly invisible in the darkness. The branches of huge, ancient oak trees rose like giant umbrellas over the house, as if they were intent on protecting it.

There were other boulders circling the lawn, all smaller than the one that had attacked them, but there was no sign that any of them were precariously perched.

"You said you saw a light up here," Toni told Lynne accusingly. "I don't see any lights. The place looks deserted. Gives me the creeps."

"Are you kidding?" Daisy cried, moving quickly toward the back of the house. "Ever hear the expression, beggars can't be choosers?

It's shelter, isn't it? I wouldn't care if it was Dracula's castle, it's got a roof and four walls and unless that roof leaks, it's dry inside. Let's go!"

"It'll be locked," Molloy said, but she hurried after Daisy. The rain was coming down hard again, pounding on her slicker as if it wanted to get in. Every step she took in her mud-encrusted flats was like sloshing through the creek all over again. "But if we can get in, I can use the phone to call Ernie and he'll come and get us. He'll take us back to the car to get our stuff, and then to the dorm. The thought of a hot shower, warm towels, and dry clothing seems like heaven. Let's just hope this back door isn't locked."

It was. Firmly. There was no screen door, but the wooden door, the upper half glass, the frame freshly painted white, was unyielding.

Lynne groaned in disappointment. Molloy shrugged as if to say, Well, of course it's locked. Who would go away and leave their doors unlocked? Toni said from behind them, "I don't see how we could just walk into someone's house, anyway. Why don't we go out front and see if there's a main road out there that's not flooded?"

"I am not," Daisy said, moving away from them, "going *anywhere* until I dry off, is that clear?" She was back a moment later, a large rock in her right hand. Daisy gave the windowpane closest to the doorknob a sharp rap with the rock. The glass cracked evenly down the middle of the pane. Another tap, and the glass caved inward, tinkling gently as the broken pieces landed on the floor inside the house.

The hole Daisy had created in the door window was relatively free of jagged edges. She stuck her hand inside without hesitation. "There's a chain, too," she said when she had turned the latch. "That'll be trickier, but I think I can get it."

A moment later they were standing inside a long, narrow, dark kitchen, in a house so quiet, the sound of the rain attacking the windows seemed as loud as a dentist's drill.

"It's empty," Lynne said almost in a whisper. "I can tell. It *smells* empty, like no one's cooked any food in this kitchen for a while. And it *feels* empty. You know, like when you're the last person riding on a bus late at night? That kind of empty."

"We shouldn't be in here," Tony said, glancing around anxiously. "We're breaking the law."

"We're cold and we're wet and we're lost," Daisy replied, moving around the kitchen in search of a towel, "so the laws don't apply to us right now. When I am wearing dry clothes, I will once again become the law-abiding, responsible citizen I have always been. Somebody find a light switch. I can't see a thing. This is a kitchen; it has to have at least *one* towel."

Using her flashlight, the beam dying again, Lynne found an oversized denim jacket hanging on a hook just inside the back door. She plucked it from the rack with glee, then turned to ask if anyone else wanted it.

Everyone was wet and cold. But Lynne looked worse than anyone else, in her thin, saturated T-shirt. "No," they all said in a chorus, "you put it on."

Lynne found a bedroom door just off the kitchen, handed Molloy the fading flashlight, and went inside. When she came back out a moment later, she was wearing the dry denim jacket over an ugly, print, cotton dress. "I found it hanging on the back of the door," she said, laughing and holding the hem of the dress away from her sides. "Horrendous, isn't it? But it was dry, and frankly, it feels wonderful." On her feet, she wore equally ugly black felt slippers. "Anybody got a camera?" she joked. "We could do one of those 'Don't' pictures for a fashion magazine."

"Are there other clothes in there?" Daisy asked, heading for the door.

Although the bedroom closet and dresser drawers were stripped almost bare, everyone found something dry to wear. Molloy shed her dripping clothing, replacing it with a bulky, worn gray cardigan with two missing buttons, and a pair of gray pants so large she had to tie the cord from Daisy's windbreaker hood around her waist to hold them up. Daisy unearthed a long-sleeved, wine velvet dress from a trunk at the foot of the bed. It was a good deal smaller than the clothes Molloy and Lynne had found, and smelled as if it had been in the trunk a very long time. Toni had to settle for a long-sleeved white shirt that hung to her knees.

Their most welcome discovery was a drawer stuffed full of old socks. Every sock had at least one hole in it, but they were warm and dry, and no one complained.

Thus attired, they left the bedroom, their spirits refreshed by the dry, if bizarre, clothing.

Lynne's flashlight was dying again. Molloy used it anyway, to locate a light switch on the kitchen wall just inside the door to other rooms. She flicked it once, twice, three times. Nothing happened.

"Either the people who lived here have gone

away for vacation and turned off the electricity before they left," she announced, "or they've just gone to town but the storm has taken down some wires." She frowned. "I hope they're on vacation, because if the storm took out the electricity, it could have taken out the phone, too. And the phone is what we need the most."

"Not me," Daisy said, opening and closing drawers, "a towel is what I need the most. My hair's dripping down the back of my neck. It's going to get my chic new outfit all wet." When she didn't find a towel, she gave up on the cabinets and moved to the refrigerator. "I'm starved. I'll bet there isn't a single thing to eat in this place."

She was right, the refrigerator was empty. Without electricity, the small bulb protruding from the back wall didn't come on when Daisy opened the door, but she didn't need light to realize there was nothing inside but a small, opened box of baking soda.

"It doesn't matter," Molloy told a crestfallen Daisy. "We're not going to be here long enough to eat. I'll call Ernie, and we'll be out of here. He'll feed us. But first, we have to find a phone."

Using the flashlight to guide their way, Molloy and Lynne left Daisy and Toni in the kitchen while they went in search of a telephone.

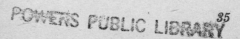

"This place is ancient," Lynne commented as they made their way along a narrow hall, its hardwood floor dotted with worn scatter rugs. "I love old houses, although I guess I've never been in one as dark and dreary as this one." She peered into every room.

There was a gigantic dining room furnished with a long, oval antique table and twelve chairs, a sideboard adorned with a bowl of dusty artificial fruit, and a built-in hutch in one corner. The library was equally good-sized, with floor-to-ceiling bookshelves and a fireplace. Heavy maroon draperies hung on the long, narrow windows. Equally heavy cloths draped over the larger pieces of furniture answered their earlier question. The people occupying the house hadn't simply gone into town to buy eggs and milk and a newspaper.

Lynne was inspecting the living room, its furniture draped with more white cloths, when Molloy found a telephone, perched on a small table near the entrance to a steep, wooden staircase in the entry hall. She snatched it up gratefully.

She had automatically begun to dial Ernie's number at the dorm when she realized with a sinking heart that there was no dial tone. The line was dead.

A loud groan of disappointment escaped her.

Hearing the sound, Lynne moved to Molloy's side. "Not the phone, too?"

Molloy nodded and reluctantly replaced the receiver. "I thought it would be so easy," she said heavily. "I'd call Ernie, he'd come and get us, take us to the car to get our things, and in no time at all, we'd be sitting in dry clothes at one of the places Ernie told me about. Vinnie's, for pizza, or Burgers, Etc., or maybe he'd even take us into town for Chinese." She sent Lynne a defeated look. "What do we do now?"

"Well, first," Lynne said briskly, "we should figure out where we are. How far from campus this place is. We can't make a plan until we know that. I mean, if it's not too far, we could walk there when the rain lets up."

"*If* the rain lets up," Molloy said, following Lynne back along the hallway toward the kitchen. "What if it doesn't? I'm not keen on camping out here all night long. I agree with Toni. There's something about this place that makes my skin crawl. And I *don't* think it's just the weather."

Lynne strode on purposefully ahead of Molloy. "Oh, you two! It's just an old house, that's all."

But a moment later, when they heard the noise, it was Lynne who whirled in fright, Lynne's face that drained of all color. "What was that?" she cried.

Molloy stood perfectly still. "I don't know. It came from up there." She pointed upward. "From upstairs. Didn't it?" she added uncertainly. She had been lost in thought, dreading the possibility of having to spend the night in this damp, dreary old place, and although the sound from above had penetrated her thoughts, she wasn't sure what kind of sound it had been.

Or had it only been thunder?

But it wasn't thundering outside. That was just rain out there, not an electrical storm. There had been no lightning, no booming thunderclaps.

Lynne, her face still pale, nodded. "I think it did come from upstairs." Her voice was so low, Molloy had to strain to hear her. "Do you think there's someone here?"

Molloy shook her head. "No one but us. You said it yourself, the place *feels* empty. The furniture's draped, the doors are locked. What we heard was probably just the wind. You know these old houses. They're full of weird drafts."

These old houses. . . . Molloy paused, lost in thought, remembering something that Ernie had told her. Something about an off-campus dorm.

She hurried back to the little table in the hall, lifted a thin, yellow-covered telephone book from beneath the phone, and glanced at the name on the cover. "Twin Falls and Surrounding Area," it read.

Salem University was in the town of Twin Falls. At least they were somewhere in the vicinity of the college.

But there was another name, neatly written in red-ink script directly beneath the heading.

"You'll be happy to know we're in the ballpark," Molloy told Lynne in a subdued voice. She glanced around, her eyes taking in the steep, old-fashioned staircase, the heavy, wooden door, the windows in the entry hall with their worn lace curtains, then the wide arch leading to the library, and an identical arch across the hall leading to the "parlor." When her gaze returned to the second heading written on the telephone cover, she said in that same somber voice, "But you might not be nearly as happy to know that we might have been better off if we'd kept going, like Toni wanted us to."

Lynne drew in her breath sharply. "Why? What's wrong? Is something wrong?"

"I think I know where we are." Molloy pointed with the tip of one finger. "See that? It's the name of this place. Nightingale Hall, it says so right there. Unless I'm remembering wrong, we're in an off-campus dorm Ernie told me about, down the road from campus, up on a hill overlooking the highway, he said."

Relief flooded Lynne's face. "Well, that's great! That's practically as good as being *on* campus, isn't it? I mean, I know this place is deserted right now, but it's still a part of the university, right? So it's not like we broke into someone's private home, after all."

"I guess so." Molloy bent to replace the phone book. When she straightened up, she added, her face serious, "But it might have been better if we had. There's a nickname for this place, Lynne. Ernie told me. Because of the terrible things that have happened in this house."

Lynne leaned against the wall, dread rising anew in her eyes. "I don't want to hear this, do I? What's the nickname, Molloy? Tell me!"

"I want to know, too," Daisy's voice came out of the hall darkness. "You guys were gone so long, we decided to feel our way through this moldy old place to find you." Toni was right behind her, following so closely they looked like one person. "So what is it, Molloy? What does everyone on campus call this damp and dreary hellhole?"

"Nightmare Hall," Molloy answered reluctantly. "They call this place Nightmare Hall."

Chapter 6

Damn! The boulder was a waste of time and I practically broke my back pushing it over to the edge of the hill. Even when the boulder didn't work, I figured they'd run back down the hill to their car. But oh, no.

I ran back inside by my secret entrance and watched from the upstairs window. Couldn't see very well, too dark, too rainy, but I could make them out, coming up over the crest of the hill. I thought maybe when they saw how creepy this place was, they'd chicken out. Steer clear of it, go around, out to the highway. But they saw shelter, and went for it.

Now what am I supposed to do? Lay low, until they go? And hope they aren't smart enough to figure out they're not in this house alone?

That's what dear old Dr. Leo would tell me to do, if he were still alive and kicking. He'd say, in that bone-dry voice of his, "Now, we need to hold it together here, right, my friend?" I hated it when he called me that. He wasn't my friend. He never understood anything about me. And he'd say, "It isn't their fault they stumbled onto your little hideaway, now, is it? So it wouldn't be right to punish them. Just keep it together until these four girls leave, and there'll be no problem."

But they might not leave. And it *is* their fault! They're the ones who broke in, who intruded, who destroyed my peaceful privacy.

I didn't break anything, the way they did. Didn't even break the padlock on the outside cellar door. Just picked it open. Found an extra set of keys hanging on that peg rack inside the back door, locked all the doors from the inside and pocketed the keys. That's something, me having the keys. I'll need them.

If I laid low and didn't let on that I was here and just let them leave, how could I be sure they hadn't seen or heard something while they were in the house? Something that wouldn't mean much to them until they heard about Dr. Leo. Then maybe they'd start to think. They might put two and two together and . . .

I can't take that chance.

Oh, no, did they hear that?

Stand still, don't make another sound. Knew

that chair was there, wasn't paying attention, ran right into it. Don't pick it up yet, let it lay there, don't move, don't even breathe. Maybe they'll think it was thunder.

No, they won't. When have I ever been that lucky?

Well, I can't let them go now. That sound alone is enough to fry me if they remember hearing it after they get to campus and find out what happened to the eminent psychologist, Dr. Milton Leo.

I guess that makes me the warden of their prison, doesn't it? Well, it's not like I was going anywhere until the roads cleared.

They'll be sorry they ever came near this place.

They don't know it, but they're my captives now. Forever.

It's not my fault.

They shouldn't have broken in here.

Their fault, not mine. Never mine.

I'd better get started. I'm going to be very, very busy.

Chapter 7

"Nightmare Hall?" Toni said, her eyes wide. "This place is called Nightmare Hall? Why?"

Molloy's expression was grim. "Some girl died here. Ernie didn't give me all the details. I don't think he knew exactly what happened. Whatever it was, it was bad. A murder, I think. Or maybe a suicide. And I got the impression that there was more, but he didn't want to scare me."

"Even if nothing had happened here," Lynne said, leading the way to the library, "they'd probably still call it that, because that's what it looks like. Someone's worst nightmare. It's dark now, but you can still see that getting a good night's sleep here could be a real challenge. The house is so old, it's probably full of weird noises." She glanced at Molloy. "Like the one we just heard upstairs."

"You heard a noise upstairs?" Toni asked.

"Why does anyone live here?" Daisy asked as Lynne and her anemic flashlight led them into the large, high-ceilinged room with the white-draped furniture. "I mean, if everyone thinks it's so creepy, why would they move in?"

"Because it's cheap." The room smelled damp, musty, as if the rain outside were penetrating the walls. "And it's close to campus. Besides, a lot of kids don't like living with dorm rules. There's a housemother, Ernie said, but I guess she's not all that strict. These must be her socks we're wearing."

Toni moved to stand beside the fireplace. "You guys heard a noise?" she repeated. "What kind of noise?"

"Sounded like someone had dropped something," Lynne said almost absentmindedy. She was staring at the fireplace. "Listen, why don't we have a fire?"

"*Who* dropped something?"

Lynne ignored Toni's question. "A nice, roaring fire in the fireplace would warm us up. It's a lot colder in here than it is outside, probably because the house has been closed up. Besides, someone might see smoke coming from the chimney. They'll think a fire in July is weird and come rescue us. Kind of like sending smoke signals."

"No wood," Molloy said, pointing to the fire-box beside the hearth.

"I saw some outside. I'll get it."

"You're going outside all by yourself?" Toni asked, her voice high and strained.

"The woodbox is right outside the back door, Toni. We don't need much. I'll be right back."

"You'll get wet again," Daisy said. "Put my slicker on. It's hanging on the kitchen door-knob. And don't go out there in those flimsy little black slippers. Put your shoes back on. You could step on a nail or something. And take the flashlight. We're used to the dark now. We can find our way around without it."

"I will, I will! You guys are worse than my mother."

Molloy hesitated, then said, "I'm coming with you." She moved away from what looked like a large couch under its white drape, and headed for the doorway.

"No!" Lynne said sharply. "It's silly for two of us to get wet. I'm going by myself."

There was something in her voice that stopped Molloy. She didn't understand what it was. She only knew that for whatever reason, Lynne was determined to get the wood on her own.

"Okay, okay," Molloy agreed. "Just hurry back, all right? I don't think we should be separating until we really know our way around."

Still, as she turned around and joined Daisy and Toni, both leaning against the fireplace, Molloy's uncertainty about being in Nightmare Hall grew. If everyone on campus was leery of it, as Ernie had told her, there had to be a reason. Maybe a lot of reasons.

"How could you have heard something being dropped upstairs?" Toni asked when Lynne had disappeared from the room. "We were all down here."

"Toni," Daisy huffed, "they didn't say something dropped. They said it *sounded* like something had dropped. Probably the wind."

"That's what we thought," Molloy agreed. "I mean, it couldn't have been anything else. The house was locked when we got here, and there's no food, so there couldn't be anyone here but us."

"Well, I say as long as we're here," Daisy said, yanking one of the cloths off a large, over-stuffed, ugly brown chair, "let's get comfy, okay? If I don't sit down right now, I'm going to keel over in front of this fireplace, and you won't be able to start a fire unless you haul me out of the way first." She plopped down on the sofa. "Sit, you guys. You make me nervous standing there."

In the kitchen, Lynne made a face of distaste

as she pulled on the wet, muddy sneakers she had shed at the back door. They squished when she took the first step. But Daisy was right. There could be wood splinters near the wood-box out back and the last thing she needed right now was a big, fat, very painful sliver of wood jamming itself into the sole of her foot.

What had she done with her baseball bat? Never mind, she couldn't carry it and the wood at the same time, anyway. And she was only going to be out there a minute or two.

She pulled Daisy's yellow slicker over her shoulders and yanked open the back door, just as the flashlight died. Lynne shook it. Nothing. Oh, well, she thought in resignation as she stepped out into the storm, having a working flashlight would be nice, but having dry shoes would be even nicer.

A wide overhang above Lynne's head pro-vided some protection from the pelting rain as she left the safety of the back porch. It was pitch black out, but she remembered the wood-box being slightly to the right of the porch steps. Her heart pounded with a mixture of fear and excitement when she moved toward the box.

Rain dripped steadily from the eaves as Lynne dropped the useless flashlight on the ground, lifted the woodbox lid, and bent from the waist to search for the right-sized log.

Her fingers had just wrapped themselves around a medium-sized chunk of wood when she heard soft, wet footsteps rushing up behind her. Her head turned to the right to see who it was.

A hand reached out from behind her and plucked a thick log from the woodbox.

"Molloy?" Lynne said.

The log slammed against her right temple. She let out a soft, distressed sigh, then her eyes closed and she slid to the cold, wet ground.

In the library, Molloy said into the musty darkness, "She should have been back by now. It shouldn't be taking her so long. All she had to do was take a few steps outside to the wood-box and grab a log or two."

"She's probably back in the kitchen, taking off her wet things," Daisy offered. Her head was back against the sofa, her eyes closed, short blonde curls tumbling across the rough brown fabric. "I hope she put my slicker on, like I told her to. And not just for her sake, either. If she doesn't cover up any log she brings in, it'll be too wet to burn. I *want* that nice, blazing fire. I can almost feel it."

Molloy jumped to her feet. "I think we should go help. I know she said not to, but maybe she couldn't get the woodbox lid open. Come on."

Groaning, Toni and Daisy left the couch, although Daisy grumbled the whole time they were making their way down the unlit hallway to the kitchen.

Lynne wasn't there, shedding wet clothing. She wasn't on the back porch, either.

"See, I told you," Molloy said, moving onto the porch to peer out. "I'll bet anything she couldn't get that lid open. And she's so stubborn, she's probably still trying. We have to go help."

"We'll get drenched again!" Daisy complained. "And there aren't any more dry clothes in that bedroom."

"Just stay as close to the house as you can. It's only a few steps, Daisy."

But staying close to the house didn't help. The wind had picked up again, whistling eerily around the house, driving the rain straight at the trio as they ran to the woodbox.

There was no one there. No one standing at the box or near the box or behind the box. No Lynne.

"Here's her flashlight," Toni said, bending to pick it up. She flicked it on, and was rewarded with a faint but steady beam of light.

"Lynne?" Molloy raised one arm to shield her

head from the blowing rain. "Lynne, where are you?"

There was no answer.

"Where did she go?" Toni's voice was barely audible above the whistling wind.

"There!" Daisy cried suddenly, "there, on the ground." She pointed, and Molloy and Toni's eyes moved in that direction. Toni aimed the flashlight.

One very wet, very muddy, hot-pink sneaker lay on its side at the base of the woodbox.

But the girl who had been wearing that sneaker was gone.

Chapter 8

They're mine now. I can't let any of them go. Here they are, and here they'll stay . . . forever.

Laying low and letting them leave unaware of my presence would have been impossible. I knew that all along, but when I heard them talking about building a fire, I knew then that they didn't intend to leave any time soon. Planned to set up camp, did they? Like they owned the place. I had no choice. I couldn't have stayed hidden and quiet all night long.

Suppose I had decided to spare them? There was no way I could let them build a fire. A fire! In July? The first person who noticed smoke coming from the chimney at Nightingale Hall would call 911 and this place would be surrounded by shrieking fire trucks and police cars in minutes.

I had to stop that girl. It was her own fault. Stupid, stupid girl. She deserved what she got.

This is my place! They have no right to waltz in here and take over, ruining things for me.

One down, three to go.

But first, I have to make sure they can't get out. That's crucial. Because now that their friend is missing, one of them is going to want to run for help.

I can't let that happen.

I won't.

Chapter 9

When Molloy called Lynne's name again, and then again, there was rising panic in her voice. Her shout disappeared into the darkness and wind and rain without reply.

No one said anything. They stood under the useless overhang, so lost in fear for their friend that they were completely unaware of the wind and the rain.

"She isn't *here*," Daisy said. "How can she not be here? She *has* to be here." She moved out from under the overhang then, her wet and filthy socks making a sloshing sound on the grass as she darted through the pouring rain from one bush to another, one bed of flowers to another, one tree to another, calling Lynne's name.

"Daisy, come back!" Toni cried, tears of terror spilling from her eyes. "You don't know what's out there, please, come back! Oh, what is going on?" she wailed. "Where is Lynne?"

Daisy came back, her thin shoulders hunched against the rain. "She's not out there."

Molloy's eyes returned to the woodbox. She took the flashlight from Toni and played it over the big, square wooden container. "What are those spots?" she said almost to herself, her voice quavering. "There, on the woodbox." She took a step forward, reached out, touched one of the spots with the tip of a finger, held the finger under the flashlight, gasped when she saw the color. Red. Pale with rainwater, but still red. Recoiling in revulsion, she said softly, "It's blood! It's blood. Something horrible has happened to Lynne out here."

"Blood?" Toni gasped. "Are you sure?"

Frantically wiping her finger on the gray pants, Molloy nodded. Her face was the same color as the pants. "I never should have let her come out here alone."

"It wasn't just you," Daisy said. "We let her go alone, too, because we didn't want to get wet again." She glanced at the dark spatters on the woodbox, and shivered. "An animal?" she said, her eyes returning to Molloy. "Do you think an animal attacked Lynne?"

"No." Molloy was so cold, wet, and frightened, her teeth had begun to chatter. "Ernie said this place was close to campus. So we're not out in the wilderness. There wouldn't be any wild animals around."

"Then what?" Toni asked breathlessly. "What happened to Lynne?"

"I don't know." Molloy glanced around fearfully and took several steps backward, toward the house. "I . . . I don't know how to say this, except to say it. I'm . . . I'm starting to wonder if the ground really did give way under that boulder. Maybe . . . maybe someone gave it some help."

It took a few moments for that frightening thought to sink in. When it had, Daisy and Toni, their terror-stricken eyes scanning the dark emptiness surrounding the house, took their own steps backward.

"You think there's someone out here?" Toni whispered, her hand on Molloy's sweater sleeve. "Someone who hurt Lynnie? Why would someone hurt her? Or push a boulder down on top of us? We don't even *know* anyone around here. Except Ernie."

"I don't know." Three pair of eyes frantically scanned the darkness even as their feet continued to move backward, toward the porch. "But if Lynne hurt herself on the woodbox somehow, she wouldn't run off. She'd come back inside the house."

"Maybe she did." Daisy's head turned toward the house. "Maybe we just didn't hear her. If she hurt herself, cut her hand or something, she could have come straight inside and into that bedroom to look for a Band-Aid. Let's go inside and look."

"I think we should get away from here," Toni said urgently. "She's not in the house. We would have heard her come in."

Molloy spoke softly, quietly, firmly. "We can't leave now, not with Lynne missing. We can't just abandon her. She has to be around here somewhere." She glanced around again, although she could see nothing. "If we're right about that boulder being pushed down the hill on top of us, we shouldn't even be out here. I think we'd better get back inside, right this second. We can decide what to do once we're safe in the house . . . with the door *locked*."

Toni pulled back. "I think we should go for help," she said stubbornly.

Daisy whirled on her. "How far do you think we'd get before the same thing that happened to Lynne happened to us?"

Toni looked stunned. "Don't *say* it like that, Daisy. We don't *know* what happened to Lynne."

Daisy's eyes flew to the dark spots on the woodbox. "Well, if she's not in the house, we'll know it wasn't anything good, won't we?" she snapped and, grabbing Toni's elbow, yanked her forward. "We are *going* inside and you're coming with us. Before you disappear, too."

Although what they all really wanted to do when they were safely inside the house was conduct an immediate search for their missing friend, Daisy insisted they take some precautions first. They closed the back door, but could only slip the chain in place. The lock required a key they didn't have. With the aid of the flashlight, Daisy found a roll of duct tape in a kitchen drawer and for want of anything better, taped a frying pan over the hole in the window. "If there is someone out there," she said, staring at her crude handiwork, "and he punches the frying pan out of that hole, we will be able to hear it."

While Daisy was working on the door, Molloy searched the kitchen drawers and was rewarded when her fingers encountered a brand-new package of batteries, the proper size for the flashlight. She hurriedly inserted them, switched the light on, and the kitchen came to life.

If they hadn't been frantic about their missing friend, they would have cheered.

Still, it would be easier to look for her now.

Then, walking very quietly and very close

together, their clothes dripping a wet trail on the floor as they went, they made their way from room to room, searching for Lynne. The darkness was broken only by the yellow glow of the revitalized flashlight.

There was no sign of their missing friend on the first floor. On the second and third floors, the rooms were neat but vacant. Molloy found herself scrutinizing the white floor tile in the bathrooms for telltale drops of blood. There were none. Bitter disappointment washed over her. Instead of being relieved that Lynne wasn't standing at the sink bandaging a cut hand, Molloy felt cold fingers of fear clutching at her throat, making it hard for her to swallow. Lynne hadn't been in any of the bedrooms, and now she wasn't in any of the bathrooms, either. Molloy didn't want to think about what that meant, but she had to.

Molloy saw her own fear reflected in Toni's eyes. "She isn't here," Toni said softly. "She's *not*. What's happened to her?"

"There's still the attic," Daisy said, reaching for the knob on a wooden door at one end of the third floor hall. "Maybe she went up there looking for dry clothes. It's an attic. It'll have clothes, right?" She waved the dripping hem of her wine velvet dress. "We could all use something dry to wear, so we might as well check it out."

"She wouldn't have come up here alone, would she?" Toni asked. But she followed close behind Daisy and Molloy as they made their way up the narrow staircase, calling out Lynne's name as they went.

Nothing answered them but the sound of rain hitting the roof.

The attic, smelling faintly musty with a hint of lavender, was breathtakingly hot. The small, squat windows set low in one wall were closed, and the air was stale. The large space was crammed full of old furniture, boxes, and trunks, and there was a door set into one wall.

Daisy stalked over to it and yanked it open. "Lynne? Are you in there?" She yanked on a chain hanging from the low ceiling inside the closet. "There are clothes in here," she called over her shoulder. "In garment bags. We'll find something, we'll change, and then we'll retrace our steps, only we'll look harder this time. I still think Lynne's in the house somewhere."

"I don't," Toni said almost in a whisper.

Molloy didn't, either. But saying aloud that Lynne had not come back inside the house would mean that Lynne hadn't been *able* to come back inside the house. That was such a totally revolting thought that Molloy couldn't bring herself to voice it. Giving voice to it would have granted it harsh reality.

Not yet, she told herself, choking back panic, not yet. I can't.

Daisy began yanking clothes from hangers in the garment bags, tossing them out of the closet. "Pick what you want," she muttered from the closet depths, "but hurry up! We don't want Lynne to come back inside and find *us* missing."

Toni rolled her eyes and whispered to Molloy, "I never thought of Daisy as being the least bit unrealistic, but right now she sounds like Lynne just went out for a nice little walk around the block."

"C'mon, Toni, let's just find some dry clothes."

Molloy had just dumped her soaked clothing in a heap on the wooden floor and slipped into an antique, very yellowed white blouse with long sleeves and a high collar and a long black skirt, when the pounding began. "What was that? Did you hear that?"

"What was what?" Daisy emerged from the closet. "I couldn't find anything to wear. And all I hear is rain. Sounds like it's going to hammer itself right through the roof, doesn't it?"

Molloy continued to listen. "Maybe that's

what I heard. No, there it is again. Listen!"

Toni was tying the belt around the waist of a faded navy and yellow print dress. It was at least three sizes too big for her. She lifted her head to listen and, a moment later, said, "That's not the rain. It's . . . it's *real* hammering." She frowned. "It sounds awfully close."

They stood close together, listening in silence. Daisy aimed the flashlight at the stairs, as if she expected the source of the hammering to be revealed there.

"Lynne!" Toni cried, her face lighting up. "It must be Lynne hammering! She came back in to start the fire and the damper on the fireplace is stuck. She's pounding on it with something to get it open." She grabbed at Molloy's wrist. "Come on, let's get down there, before she thinks *we're* missing."

"It's not Lynne," Daisy said curtly. "She would have come looking for us before she'd try to start a fire. It's a loose shutter banging in the wind, that's all. And nobody's going anywhere until I've found something dry to wear. I'm so drenched I'm surprised I haven't sprouted scales."

Molloy and Toni looked uncertain. "It doesn't sound like a loose shutter," Toni said.

"Sure, it does. And as far as I'm concerned, it can bang itself silly. I only have two things on my mind: finding Lynne, and finding some dry clothes."

"I guess it does sound a little like a flapping shutter," Molloy said as Daisy moved to a large, antique trunk sitting against one wall.

"No, it doesn't," Toni disagreed. "It sounds like hammering. But I know it couldn't be, because we're all up here, and Lynne wouldn't be down there with a hammer and nails, so I guess it has to be a loose shutter." But she didn't look convinced.

"Hurry up, Daisy!" Molloy chided as Daisy fumbled with the lock on the trunk. "Maybe Toni's right. Maybe we just missed Lynne somehow and she's been in the house the whole time. This is a huge house. There could even be a back staircase somewhere. She could have been going in one direction while we were going in another. We'll all be cracking up when we get downstairs. I mean," she added with false brightness because she really didn't believe a word she was saying, "wouldn't that be hilarious?"

Just then, Daisy got the trunk open and lifted the lid.

And instead of laughing at the thought of thinking that Lynne was missing when she'd been in the house the whole time, Daisy stumbled backward, her hands flew to her mouth, and she let out a high, piercing scream.

The scream hung in the musty air under the low-hanging attic rafters as Toni and Molloy, their cheekbones white with fear, ran to Daisy's side.

"Don't look," Daisy gasped, her hands still at her mouth, "don't, it's horrible!"

But their eyes were already on the contents of the trunk.

Toni moaned, and clutched at Daisy for support.

"Oh, no," Molloy breathed, "no."

Inside the trunk, curled up peacefully on a thick pile of neatly folded blankets, lay Lynne Grossman. Her eyes were closed. Her short, dark hair and her clothes were still wet and had created a dark, damp spot encircling her on the pile of bedding. She was wearing only one hot-pink, very muddy sneaker.

She was lying so still, her features so calm and composed, that it would have looked as if she were merely taking a quick catnap except for one significant, sickening detail.

There was a large, ugly wound on Lynne Grossman's right temple.

Chapter 10

So they found her. That scream was loud enough to make the grass stop growing.

It doesn't matter. It's not like I was planning to let them leave, anyway. So who are they going to tell about their friend being stuffed into a trunk in the attic? No one.

It's not my fault. Because if they hadn't heard or seen anything while they were in the house, I could have let them go. They wouldn't have had anything to tell anyone about this place, except that it was creepy.

But after the chair fell, I could just hear one of them saying to the police, "Well, officer, now that you mention a murder, I do remember hearing a noise when we were inside Nightmare Hall. It sounded like someone upstairs had dropped something on the floor. So maybe you should check the place out."

There's just no way I can let them go.

I'd better finish what I'm doing here. It's going faster than I'd expected. Good thing, because any second now, someone will come racing down those steps to see if the phone is working yet, so they can call an ambulance for their surprise package in the trunk.

Just a few more nails . . .

Chapter 11

At ten minutes after nine, Ernie Dodd called the state police to see if any accidents had been reported on the highway between Briscoe and Twin Falls.

The answer was negative, with a follow-up of, "No accidents because most of that highway's closed, due to flooding. We've been warning people since seven o'clock this evening to stay off the road.

"Wouldn't be too many people out there tonight, anyway," the officer added. "What with a killer on the loose. I figure most people around here have their doors and windows locked up tight right about now. The guy's going to be looking for a safe haven, and he'll take it wherever he can find it, even if that means breaking in." He uttered a short, humorless laugh. "What's breaking and entering compared to murder, right?"

"Right," Ernie agreed. But he was thinking that Molloy and Lynne, Daisy and Toni wouldn't *know* about the murder. Unless they'd heard it on the car radio before they'd travelled very far. If they had, maybe that news, combined with the bad weather, had led them to postpone their trip for at least a day. If it had, Molloy would be home now.

Gearing up his courage, Ernie went to the phone again. This time, he was greeted by a sporadic dial tone. There was a lot of static on the line, and he wasn't sure how long it would be operational. Consoling himself with the thought that the only reason he hadn't heard from Molloy was the state of the telephone lines, he dialed her home phone number.

Her mother's voice was cool, as he had known it would be. "Yes, of course, they left on time. I tried to talk them into waiting until tomorrow so the weather would be better, but my daughter never listens to me."

If she did, Ernie heard, she wouldn't be dating someone like Ernie Dodd.

"Why? What's wrong?" Mrs. Book added anxiously. "Aren't they there yet? Oh, heavens, they would have to be there by now."

Ernie didn't know what to say. He didn't want to worry Molloy's parents, but he couldn't very well lie and say Molloy was there when she wasn't. "I just found out that the highway is closed," he said, "so they can't get through. They've had to stop somewhere and wait for the water to go down." He knew that sounded as if he'd actually heard from Molloy. Well, so what? There wasn't anything the Books could do if Molloy was stuck somewhere because of high water. Let them think she was safe for now.

When Molloy's mother began pressing him for details as to exactly *where* Molloy had said she was when she called him, Ernie was saved by the line going bad again. He could still hear Mrs. Book's voice over a blend of crackling and spitting noises, but he couldn't make out what she was saying. He hung up.

Someone knocked on his door and, for just a split second, Ernie had the eerie feeling that Mrs. Book had magically transported herself to Devereaux dorm and was standing outside his door waiting for answers to her questions.

It was Ernie's friend Simon, a tall, lanky baseball player. His hair was drenched, his face dripping, his windbreaker and jeans clinging to him. He was with his fellow baseball player, Elise Cook. Tall, blonde, and broadshouldered, her short blonde hair was wet, and neatly combed into place, as if she'd just taken a shower. Her jeans and Salem T-shirt were dry. Elise lived at Devereaux. Simon didn't.

"You were out in this?" Ernie asked Simon, letting them in.

"No other way to get here, pal. Couldn't find any underground tunnels. You hear about Leo?" Simon asked, shedding his windbreaker and reaching into the bathroom for a towel. Unwilling to sit in his wet clothes, he leaned agaínt the bathroom doorframe. "The police are all over campus. One guy told me they think it was one of Leo's patients. That includes us, Ernie. They'll be knocking on our doors any minute now."

Elise slouched in Ernie's desk chair, long legs stretched out in front of her, silently watching as Ernie sat down on the bed and looked at Simon in surprise. "Knocking on my door? I only saw Leo that one time. When I was feeling so bummed about being away from Molloy. I told you guys about it."

Elise nodded. "I remember."

"He wasn't much help," Ernie continued. "Talked about something called codependence and never said a single word about love." He didn't add that he had, in fact, become so angry with Dr. Leo he had shouted, and his secretary had stuck her nose into the office to see if anything was wrong, meaning should she run to the phone and place a call to campus security?

His name would probably be right at the top of the list of patients she handed over to the police. "I didn't go back and I don't consider myself one of his patients. You didn't see him that much, either, did you?" he asked Simon.

"Just twice. But my name's in his files. I guess the word'll get out now, won't it? I wonder what people will say? Macho baseball player sees shrink over an allergic reaction to his new baseball uniform. Anyway, he wasn't helping me. That's why I only saw him twice."

"I saw him more than that," Elise volunteered. "For my insomnia. And he did help. Arthur recommended him."

Simon laughed rudely. "Arthur? You did something Arthur recommended?"

"It helped." Elise began nervously running her fingers through her cropped hair. "I was off my game because I wasn't getting enough sleep. Arthur said he never went a single day without seeing Dr. Leo, so I thought I'd give it a try." To Simon, she said with dread in her voice, "You think that we're all suspects? Just because we were patients of his?"

Simon shrugged. "Looks that way."

Ernie began pacing back and forth in front of the rain-streaked window. "What really bothers me," he said in a low, urgent voice, "what is *really* driving me nuts, is that Molloy is out there and they haven't caught that guy. I mean, isn't he going to be looking for a ride out of town? The state police said there was almost no one on the road. If Lynne got stubborn, and kept going when she shouldn't have, and if they're just about the only car on the road, they could come across that maniac and he'll want their car."

Simon frowned. "Molloy's not here yet? I thought you told me she was supposed to be here by six. We," he said glancing toward Elise, "were going to take you two out to eat. Although after practically swimming over here from my dorm, I think we'll have to settle for the cafeteria downstairs, gruesome though that prospect is."

"She *was* supposed to be here by six. I just wish I knew for sure that they'd stopped somewhere, a motel or something. Maybe she tried to call and couldn't get through."

"It does seem like she'd have called to tell you where she is," Elise said.

"The phones are really bad. Some of the lines are down and even where they aren't, there's so much interference, you can't hear the other person. I know because I just talked to Molloy's mother." Ernie forced a wan grin. "Nobody I'd rather be talking to when the line goes dead."

Simon laughed. But he was serious again almost immediately. "So, what are you going to do? About Molloy, I mean?"

"I don't know." Ernie was a writer. He had a very vivid imagination. That imagination had dredged up a terrifying image of Molloy sitting in a car stranded in high water as some crazy maniac with wild eyes approached from behind. "But if I don't do something, I'm going to go nuts! Any ideas?"

"State police."

"Already called them. They said no reported accidents. So at least I know she's not lying in some emergency room somewhere." Ernie had resumed his pacing.

Simon moved to stand behind Elise's chair. "Maybe they've finally caught the guy. I'd kind of like to get a good night's sleep, know what I mean?"

"Wouldn't have to be a guy," Elise said, as if she were thinking aloud.

"What?"

"I said what makes you think it was a guy? Why couldn't it have been a girl? I'm not Leo's only female patient. There are others. Girls who saw him a lot more often than I did. Becca Turnbull, for one, and she acted like she hated him. And Corinne Summerson. She's an athlete, and big enough and strong enough to bash in someone's skull. Except I think she had a crush on Dr. Leo. She couldn't wait to see him every day. Like Arthur."

Simon reached into an open box of cookies Ernie's mother had sent, sitting on top of Ernie's stereo. "I've been thinking about Arthur," Simon said.

Ernie stared at him. "Arthur? Arthur *Banks*?"

Simon took a huge bite out of the cookie. "Um-hum. He's pretty weird, Ernie. You gotta admit that. I mean, how many other guys do you know who wear suspenders even with shorts?"

"We're going to hang this guy on the basis of his wardrobe?"

Simon shook his head. Cookie crumbs flew. "It's not just that. He saw Leo every day, Ernie. He told us that, when I was talking about my allergy, remember? 'I couldn't function without Dr. Leo's help,' was what Arthur had to say. 'A day without a visit to Dr. Leo would be a dark day for me.' That's actually what weird old Arthur said."

"Well, then, he certainly wouldn't have killed him, would he, Simon?" Elise said tartly. "Arthur's okay. He's just . . . strange, that's all." She shrugged. "Who isn't?"

Impatient with them, Ernie said, "Look, I don't want to talk about this anymore, okay? I have to find out where Molloy is. That's all I care about right now." He moved to the door, picking up his baseball jacket as he passed his bed. "I'm going to go talk to the police. I want to know what they're doing to find that head case. And maybe they can help *me* find out where Molloy is."

Simon straightened up, pocketed several more cookies, and nodded. "Yeah, sure, Ernie. But can we eat first? My stomach is howling with hunger. A few more minutes won't hurt, will it?"

"You two go ahead. I'm not hungry."

"Okay if we come back up here and wait for you after we eat?" Elise asked. "I want to know what you found out."

"Sure. But you'll have to wait in the hall, because I'm locking the door. Can't have some crazy killer using my room as a hideout, can I?"

The three separated on the ground floor, and as Ernie left the building he remembered what Simon had said. "A few more minutes won't hurt."

Didn't that depend on where Molloy was and what was happening to her?

How many minutes had it taken for Dr. Leo's head to be crushed?

Chapter 12

In the attic at Nightingale Hall, Toni was the first to cry out, "Oh, God, what happened to Lynne? Look at her head! She's bleeding! Is she dead?" Her eyes darted frantically around the dark, cluttered attic, as if she expected someone to jump out from behind the boxes and trunks and furniture. Her voice hushed almost to a whisper, she said, "Someone *is* out there! Lynne didn't cut herself on the woodbox. That blood we saw was from that awful wound on her head."

Looking dazed, Daisy nodded. "And she didn't hit herself over the head and throw herself in this trunk. Someone else did."

They stood very close together, their eyes scanning the attic in dread, their breath coming in short, anxious gasps.

"This is unreal," Daisy said, staring down at Lynne. "How could someone have brought her into the house and up here without any of us hearing or seeing him? Up all those stairs . . ."

"Oh, no," Toni whispered, her hands clutching the edge of the trunk, "he's *in* here! He's in the house!" Words spilled out of her mouth as panic overtook her. "He's not outside, he's in *here* somewhere, with us, and there's something wrong with him or he wouldn't have done that to Lynne; he's crazy, he's got to be crazy! We don't even *know* anyone here except Ernie, so anyone who would hurt Lynne for no reason has to be crazy! What are we going to do?"

Molloy struggled to think. She couldn't believe this was happening. What had they done to make someone so angry? How had they turned themselves into targets? They had only been looking for refuge from the storm. And the place had looked so deserted.

But it wasn't, was it?

They had to get away from here. Nightmare Hall wasn't safe, just as Ernie had told her. And they had to get out . . . *fast*. He could be anywhere in the house. But first, they needed an ambulance. They couldn't just leave Lynne lying in the trunk. Minutes had to count with the kind of injury she had.

But the phones were out. What could they do? There had to be something. They couldn't just leave Lynne lying there and not do anything. They didn't even know if she was still alive.

Bending, Molloy touched Lynne's wrist. It was cool, and still damp. But it wasn't cold, as she'd been terrified it would be. She applied more pressure to the wrist. "I think I feel a pulse," she told Daisy and Toni. "Not very strong, though. It's really slow, like it's thinking about stopping any minute now. But at least she's still alive."

"Are you sure?" Daisy said.

"Yes. But we have to do something, fast." Molloy, for lack of anything better to do, swept an old, faded blue chenille bedspread from its folded spot on a chair and spread it over Lynne. "We have to get help. Help for Lynne . . . and help for *us*."

"That cut on the side of her head looks nasty," Daisy said. "Maybe we should try to clean it up. That might do her some good. I'll run downstairs and get a wet washcloth."

"Daisy!" Toni shrieked, clutching the elbow of Daisy's wine velvet dress. "You are not going down there alone! No one is. There's someone *in this house*! Someone who did *that*," pointing with a shaking finger at Lynne.

"We don't *know* that he's in here. He could be gone by now," Daisy said, without much conviction. "In fact," her voice gathering strength,

"I'll bet anything he's gone. Here's what probably happened. He was hiding in the house for some reason — maybe he's a homeless person and picked this place to get in out of the rain, just like we did. When we showed up, he decided to leave. Only when he went outside, Lynne surprised him by being at the woodbox. He panicked and hit her. Then he got scared, and decided to hide her so he'd have time to get away. Then he left." She finished on a note of satisfaction.

Toni, anxious to believe her, asked, "You really don't think he's still here?"

"Nope. There was plenty of time for him to split *before* we locked the doors. Now they're locked, so he can't get back in even if he changes his mind."

"The back door into the kitchen isn't locked," Toni reminded her. "We didn't have the key, remember? All we could do was put the chain on." She drew in her breath, almost whispering, "Maybe *he* has the key. Maybe he can come and go as he pleases."

And that was when they all realized that the loose shutter had stopped banging against the house.

Toni said it first. "The hammering . . . it's stopped."

They listened.

"But the storm hasn't," Daisy said uneasily, "so why isn't that shutter still making a racket? I mean, if it was loose before, it's still loose, right? So why isn't it still slamming away out there?"

They listened more intently.

There was no hammering sound.

"Maybe," Toni said then, leaning against an upright trunk for support because the thought she was about to give voice to made her legs weak, "maybe that hammering wasn't a loose shutter. Maybe it wasn't even coming from outside." The hand holding the flashlight dropped as if it could no longer carry the weight, and her words came out slowly, reluctantly. "Maybe . . . it . . . was . . . coming . . . from . . . inside." She stared at Molloy and Daisy. "What if he's been in here all along?"

"He *hasn't*," Daisy said, clearly struggling to convince herself as well as them. "He can't be. After he attacked Lynne, he'd get as far away from here as possible. Probably ran like the wind. It *was* a shutter we heard, and it's just stopped banging, that's all. He's not still here, so just don't say that."

"Whether he's here or not," Molloy said grimly, tucking the edges of the bedspread carefully under Lynne's chin, "we have to figure out what to do. The phones are dead. Lynne needs an ambulance, but we can't call one, and we can't call the police, either. We can't go outside because we don't want to end up like Lynne. And we can't start a fire in the fireplace so that someone will see the smoke and come running because we don't have any wood."

"Well, we can't stay up here all night, either," Daisy said. "I don't care what we do as long as we do something." She glanced down at the trunk. "We don't know how long Lynne can wait, either."

"We can't just *leave* her up here," Toni protested. "And we can't move her. Someone has to stay up here with her until help comes."

A heavy silence filled the attic. Daisy and Molloy knew Toni was right. But sitting up here with their wounded friend, necessary though it might be, wasn't going to get them away from Nightmare Hall, and it wasn't going to get them any help, either.

"I'll stay with her," Toni said suddenly, astonishing the other two girls. "You go ahead. Figure out what to do and do it, and I'll stay up here with Lynne."

"You?" Daisy gasped tactlessly.

"Daisy, I know you think of me as a whining, wimpy musician, but I think I can handle sitting with Lynne. And before you hand me any medals for bravery, I have to tell the truth. I feel safer up here, in this one room at the top of the house, than I would downstairs with all of those other rooms for someone to be hiding in."

"He's *not* still here," Daisy denied vehemently. "He's not!" But her voice trembled.

"You won't leave me in the house alone, though, right?" Toni said anxiously. "I mean, you won't suddenly decide to both go for help, will you? One of you will stay here and let me know what's going on?"

"We would never do that, Toni," Molloy said. "And before we put you on guard duty, we'll go down and get Arturo for you. Where'd you leave him?"

"I had him with me until we started up the attic stairs. He's right down there in the hall. That'd be great."

Toni grabbed at the violin case when they brought it to her as if it held all the answers. Clutching it, she huddled on the floor beside the trunk. "It's awfully stuffy in here," she complained. "I need air, and Lynne probably does, too. I'll open a window."

"Okay," Daisy said, "we'll be back up as soon as we figure out how to get out of this mess."

Toni insisted they take the flashlight. "It's not like I'm going anywhere," she said. "And you've got the whole house to deal with. I know where everything is up here, and if I bump into a box or two, it won't . . . hurt me."

Daisy and Molloy knew she had started to say, "It won't kill me."

Daisy took an extra precious few minutes to take off the damp velvet dress and throw on an old blue coat she found hanging on a peg rack against one wall. Then, with one last check on Lynne, who was still breathing but hadn't moved at all, Daisy and Molloy left the attic.

On the third floor, Daisy said quietly, "I can't believe someone carried Lynne into the house and all the way up to the attic without us knowing about it. How is that possible?"

Molloy shrugged. She kept the flashlight aimed in front of them as they cautiously made their way down the stairs. "There has to be another staircase. A lot of old houses have back stairs. We should look for it. But first we have to figure out how to get help. That's the first thing. I'm worried sick about Lynne. Her pulse was so weak."

"She's not going to die, is she?" Tough, streetwise Daisy's voice was quavering.

"We won't let her." But Molloy sounded far braver than she felt. She hadn't bought one word of Daisy's scenario about Lynne's attacker leaving the house. She wanted to believe it, more than she'd ever wanted to believe anything. But she couldn't. That hammering *had* come from inside the house, she was sure of it. It would have been fainter if it had come from outside, with the sound battling against the noise of the storm. This sound had been sharper, more distinct.

When they began moving down the main stairs to the second floor, they stopped talking, staying very close together. Molloy was slightly in the lead, still holding the flashlight. The house seemed to her darker and colder and more threatening. But she knew it wasn't the house itself. It was what might be *in* the house.

She knew they should be hurrying, racing downstairs to see if a telephone might be working now, or frantically trying to figure out what to do. But their steps on the stairs were small, hesitant, their eyes constantly scanning the darkness around them. And although Daisy wasn't actually clutching the back of Molloy's yellowed blouse, because Daisy wasn't that kind of person, it almost felt as if she were.

We are going to *have* to separate at some point, Molloy thought in despair. One of us will have to go for help if we can't use the phone. Lynne has to have medical attention.

The thought of running out into that stormy darkness where Lynne had been attacked, the possibility of ending up lying on the ground with her own skull cracked open, made Molloy's heart stop.

But someone had to go for help.

As they passed each room on the third and second floors, they opened the doors and Molloy swept the rooms with the flashlight. She had no idea what they would do if someone actually jumped out from behind a piece of furniture, maybe brandishing a weapon of some kind in their faces. But checking seemed better than just walking by the rooms as if everything were perfectly normal.

They found no sign of anything unusual in any of the rooms. No wet footprints, no open windows with the curtains blowing and the rain coming in.

When they reached the entry hall, and tried the phone, it was still dead.

To their relief, the front door was still locked, with no sign of forced entry.

"He's not in here," Daisy whispered in Molloy's ears as they moved cautiously along the hallway, "I know he's not. He's gone."

When they had checked the library and the parlor and the dining room and found nothing, and then moved on into the kitchen and found the frying pan still fastened firmly over the broken windowpane, Molloy's heart leaped with hope. Maybe Daisy was right. Maybe he had taken just a few minutes to come back into the house and, using a back entrance or staircase, hidden Lynne in the trunk to give himself more time to get away, and then had left by the same back entrance.

And maybe the hammering sound they'd heard really had been a shutter.

But they still had to figure out how to get help.

When they saw no sign of an intruder, Daisy said, "You said we're close to Salem. Somebody has to hike out of this mausoleum and get a doctor for Lynnie. I'll go." She forced a grin. "I'm the one wearing the coat, right?"

"Daisy . . . he could still be out there. Waiting for us to leave so he can have his place back."

"Oh, he's long gone by now. Probably terrified of the cops. If he wasn't scared of being caught, he wouldn't have gone to all that trouble to hide Lynne. He'd have left her lying there on the ground in the rain. He was buying himself some time, to get away."

It sounded so logical, made so much sense. And Daisy sounded so much like she knew what she was talking about.

"Well, at least go out the front way. Ernie said this house was on a hill overlooking a highway. Maybe you can flag down a car right away." Molloy hadn't forgotten that the highway had been closed due to flooding. She remembered the detour that had begun this nightmare. But she was trying desperately to sound optimistic before Daisy started out. And there was always a chance that the highway had been opened by now, although it didn't sound like the weather had improved much.

"Right," Daisy agreed. "If not, I'll hike up the highway on foot."

Daisy marched to the door and reached out to turn the doorknob. Turned, twisted it, shook it, felt all around the doorframe for another key, found none, yanked on the doorknob again, and, finally, gave the heavy wooden door a kick and turned around in defeat. "Without a key," she said flatly, "this door is not going to open."

"Well, let's look for one. Maybe there's an extra set somewhere."

They searched all around the doorframe and then went back into the kitchen to look. There was a key rack hanging near the back door, but it was empty.

"Well, I guess it's the back door, then," Daisy said, giving up on the search. "At least we know that one's open, since we couldn't lock it without a key."

Molloy knew Daisy didn't want to go out back, didn't want to have to pass the woodbox. She didn't blame her. But what choice did they have?

Daisy, her face pale, shrugged and went straight to the back door. Saying, "Here goes nothing!" she released the chain and turned the doorknob.

Although Daisy tugged on the door, it didn't open.

"What's going on?" Molloy said, moving forward to stand at Daisy's side.

Daisy went through the same ritual she'd performed on the front door, to no avail. The door was immovable.

Without even turning around, Daisy sagged against the door and said, "It's not going to open. It's either locked from the outside or nailed shut."

"Nailed shut? On the outside?"

Daisy turned around, her face red from her efforts. "That's what it feels like. There were a lot of old, deserted buildings in my neighborhood. When the absentee owners got tired of us kids hanging around their property, they came over and nailed all of the doors and windows shut." She added grimly as she walked to the sink to stare at the wall of windows behind it, "If someone had been *inside* those buildings when the boards went up over the doors and the nails went in," turning again to direct a level gaze at Molloy, "they would have been trapped."

"Trapped?" Molloy stared at Daisy. "But . . ."

"It's probably not nailed shut," Daisy said quickly. "But it sure is locked. And it wasn't when we came back in from the woodbox. I'll have to go out a window." But the look on her face was not optimistic as her eyes returned to the windows.

"Check them," Molloy urged, guessing what Daisy was thinking. "At least check them."

Daisy hauled a wooden chair over to the sink and stood on it to examine the windows. Her shoulders slumped. She turned her head toward Molloy who was standing behind her aiming the flashlight forward. "Well," Daisy said, her voice bleak, "now we know what all that hammering was."

Disbelieving, Molloy rushed to join Daisy at the sink, climbed up on the chair beside her, leaned forward anxiously to see for herself.

Every window had been nailed shut.

Daisy jumped down, hurried to the door, removed the tape holding the frying pan, peered out through the hole. "It's not barred," she said as she taped the pan back into place. "There wasn't time to nail a board across the door. But it *is* locked, which means someone has a key. Someone who doesn't want us leaving."

Then she turned around to face Molloy. Leaning against the door, her face drained of color and looking pinched, Daisy said wearily, "We can't leave. We're trapped in here."

Chapter 13

I'm in charge now.

Don't worry, you're not alone here in this dismal place. I'm here. I'm right here, listening, even watching sometimes. Like now.

The girl with the frizzy blonde hair all wet and curly around her face looks mad. The other girl, the pretty one in the long skirt, looks like a trapped animal.

They can't believe the windows are nailed shut.

They'll start looking for another way out now, but they won't find one. This is my territory, and I know my way around. Wherever they are, I'll be somewhere else. Except, of course, when I'm picking them off, one by one, like apples from a tree.

This might be fun, after all. Hadn't planned on it, of course. But now it feels kind of like a game. Entertainment for a rainy night. If they hadn't come along, what would I be doing? Hanging around this place waiting for the roads to open.

I know exactly which one to get rid of first. It'll be as easy as stealing grapes at the super-market.

Watch out, girls, here I co-ome!

Chapter 14

Ernie needed to talk to Tanner Leo. He knew it was a really crass thing to want, when her father had just been murdered, but he was going to try, anyway. Tanner might know something about the killer. She might be able to say to him, "Yes, I've already told the police who it is, but I have to tell you, Ernie, I know this guy and I promise you, he's long gone. He isn't the type to hang around waiting to get arrested."

That was what Ernie Dodd needed to hear. That the creep was long gone, and therefore no threat to Molloy.

Of course, Tanner would already have shared any information she had with the police. He should go to them instead of to the bereaved daughter. But as someone who had sought the services of Dr. Leo, Ernie Dodd was *on* that list of suspects, so he wasn't about to present himself to the police. It had to be Tanner he talked to.

Tanner played second base on the baseball team, and Ernie liked her. She was friendly and seemed helpful. Would she help him out now? Could she?

Ian Banion had said on the radio that "Dr. Leo's only survivor, his daughter, Tanner, is recovering from the news at the campus infirmary."

Ernie made his way across campus, sloshing through deep puddles as if they weren't even there.

Tanner, a tall, thin, dark-haired girl who reminded Ernie a little of Molloy, was sitting in the infirmary waiting room with Charlie Cochran, her boyfriend. He had an arm around her shoulders and was talking to her quietly, comforting her.

They looked up in surprise when Ernie walked in. He declared his condolences, which Tanner accepted with quiet gratitude, and then, sitting down, said, "Tanner, I really hate bothering you like this. I know you must be really upset."

"They gave me something," she said, gesturing toward a nurse standing behind the counter. "They tell me it'll help me sleep. I'm staying with Jodie for a few days." Jodie Lawson was Tanner's best friend. Tanner shuddered. "I couldn't go back to that house even if the police let me."

Ernie felt terrible. He shouldn't be here, bothering her like this. Then he saw a police officer in a small room off the hall, talking to a doctor. Already asking questions. They'd be coming to Ernie Dodd sooner or later to get *his* answers. Might even keep him from looking for Molloy.

He couldn't give up on Tanner. "Look, I'm sorry, Tanner. I know you must be wrecked, but I have to ask you something. I'm worried about Molloy."

Tanner knew who he meant. He had talked to everyone on the team about Molloy. "Your girlfriend? Why?"

Ernie explained. "And with that guy out there . . ."

Tanner paled.

"I thought maybe you might have some idea about who it is, and then you might also know where he might be hiding out or, better yet, where he might have escaped to," Ernie asked desperately. He knew he was grabbing at straws, but he didn't know what else to do.

"Oh, Ernie," Tanner said softly, "if I knew

who it was, don't you think I'd tell? My father and I didn't get along very well, I guess, but . . ." She bit her lower lip.

Charlie patted her shoulder and squeezed her hand.

"Think, Tanner, okay? Isn't there anything that you can think of that would help the police find this guy? I mean, he's *out* there, and for all I know, so is Molloy."

"It might not be a guy," Tanner said slowly. The sedative was beginning to hit her. "My father had female patients, too, Ernie, and some of them didn't like him very much. But I'll tell you what I told the police. If I were going to look for a fugitive, I know the first place I'd look. Nightmare Hall."

Ernie stared at her. "Nightmare Hall?" That old, gloomy brick place out on the highway, sitting up on a hill under huge, black trees. "Why there?"

"Because it's off-campus, it's out of the way, and it's empty right now. I know the house-mother has gone on vacation, and so has the handyman." She leaned closer to Charlie, and he tightened his grip around her shoulders.

"Did you tell the police to go check it out?" Ernie asked, hating himself for not leaving her alone.

Tanner nodded. "But they said right now they're busy checking every dorm, and that it would take a while. Twin Falls doesn't have a very large police force, Ernie." Her eyes began to dull from the sedative and the arm that had been resting on the chair dropped into her lap.

It was time to go. "Thanks, Tanner. Thanks for your help. And I really am sorry about what happened."

Tanner's eyes were fighting to stay open.

"I've got to get her over to Jodie's," Charlie said. He helped her upright. "I hope you find Molloy, Ernie. I'm sure she's okay."

Watching them leave, Ernie saw the way Charlie was careful to open Tanner's umbrella and shield her with it, and felt a stab of pain in his chest because he wasn't doing exactly the same thing for Molloy. He was *supposed* to be. But Molloy wasn't here.

Nightmare Hall? Was Tanner right? It *would* be the perfect place to hide out. Isolated, deserted.

It was worth a try. Even a long trek in foul weather would be worth it if Molloy opened the door to Nightmare Hall when he knocked and cried, "Ernie! You found me!"

Ernie stood up, would have bolted from the infirmary, but an authoritative voice behind him said, "Excuse me. You want to tell me your name and what you were doing talking to Dr. Leo's daughter?"

Ernie turned around to face a middle-aged, ruddy-faced policeman in uniform.

"I'm a friend of hers," he said, deliberately not giving his name. Maybe this policeman didn't know or wouldn't remember that the name 'Ernest Dodd' was on that list of suspects, probably in capital letters, but he couldn't afford to risk it. "I just came to offer my condolences."

"Nice of you." The policeman's eyes narrowed. "Coming out on a bad night like this, I mean. Could have waited till morning, right? What'd you say your name was again?"

Oh, man.

A younger officer, looking not much older than Ernie, came out of another room just then. "What's going on, Sloane?" he asked, glancing over at Ernie. "Problem?"

"Nah, no problem, Reardon. This guy was talking to the Leo girl, and now he seems to be having trouble remembering his own name."

"You want to give us your name?" the officer named Reardon asked Ernie politely. "I mean, there isn't any reason why you *wouldn't* want to, is there?"

Ernie gave up. Sometimes you could fight

City Hall, and sometimes you couldn't. This was one of those times. "Ernie Dodd," he said reluctantly.

Reardon nodded. "He's on the list," he told his partner. "Maybe that's why he wanted to keep his name to himself." To Ernie, he said, "You want to come along with us? We just have a few routine questions." He pointed into the small room. "Right in here, if you don't mind. Nothing to worry about."

Easy for you to say, Ernie thought as his earlier hope of finding Molloy soon shrivelled up and died. *Your* girlfriend isn't missing, is she?

But he moved into the room without further argument, knowing that he wasn't going to be leaving the infirmary any time soon. If Molloy *was* at Nightmare Hall, she'd have to wait a little longer for Ernie Dodd to find her.

He could only hope that she was there with no one but Lynne, Toni, and Daisy. No one else.

Not a killer looking for a place to hide.

Chapter 15

Daisy and Molloy climbed down from the chair and stood facing each other in the kitchen. The flashlight lay on the edge of the sink, its wide yellow beam casting an eerie glow across the room.

Molloy was the first to speak. "Maybe," she proposed halfheartedly, "the nails are old. Maybe the handyman did this a long time ago, to keep intruders out."

"Oh, right," Daisy said, glaring. "And he also locked the doors from the inside and pocketed the keys so we couldn't open them. And then, with the house locked up tighter than a penitentiary, he was magically transported out of here."

Molloy sagged against the sink. "Sorry. I was just trying . . ."

"You were just trying to deny the truth."

Daisy's tone softened. "I don't blame you. I was doing the same thing when I insisted that no one was in here but us." She glanced around the long, narrow, dim kitchen again, her eyes revealing raw fear now. "But someone *is*, Molloy! And for some crazy reason, he's trapped us in here with him!"

They were too bewildered to think straight. They stumbled to the round, wooden kitchen table at one end of the room and sank into chairs.

"What are we going to do?" Molloy said. She wasn't asking a question, and didn't really expect an answer. She knew Daisy was as stunned as she was. First Lynne, with that horrible wound on the side of her head, curled up inside the trunk as if she were already dead, and now this! Trapped in a horrible old house with no way out.

No, that wasn't right. That couldn't be right. Of course there was a way out. There had to be. "We'll just have to find another way out, that's all. He couldn't have nailed all of the windows shut. He didn't have time."

Daisy disagreed. "One big, fat nail, one hammer, one blow, presto, the bottom of the window frame is nailed to the windowsill and won't open. How long could it take? It's not like he had to do the upstairs windows. Who's going to jump out of a second-story window?"

But Molloy insisted they quickly check all of the first-floor windows. "If you're right, and they're all nailed shut, we'll just have to break one," she said. They had taken to talking in whispers. It seemed safer. "Then one of us has to go for help, and the other one has to get back upstairs to Lynne and Toni."

They were checking the last room, the bedroom off the kitchen, when each of them found something.

The room had no windows, and they would have turned and left quickly. But Molloy decided a coat or jacket would be helpful when one of them went out into the rain, and she opened what she thought was a closet door. Instead she found a staircase.

Daisy had her back turned, in the process of finding another pair of dry socks. She heard Molloy's gasp of discovery and whirled around, her face suffused with fear. "What? What's wrong?" Then, taking a step forward, "What is *that*?"

"It's the back staircase we talked about," Molloy said, holding the door open and peering up into the shadowed tunnel. "It was right here all along." She stared at Daisy, her eyes wide with discovery. "This is how he did it. This room is right off the kitchen. He came in the back way when we were up front in the library and carried Lynne up these stairs. He's probably been going up and down it, going in and out, the whole time we've been in here." Her eyes were huge with dismay. "Maybe even listening to us, watching us . . ." Tears of terror trembled on her eyelashes. "Oh, Daisy, he must have been so *close*! And we didn't even know it."

"Close it!" Daisy demanded, and lunged for the door, slamming it shut. "Lock it!"

Molloy stared down at the doorknob. "It doesn't lock. There's no lock. But . . ." she lifted her head, "we can put something against it. Something heavy. So he can't use the staircase anymore. Can't sneak up on us from in here." She glanced around the small, cluttered room, her eyes landing on a huge, old dresser. "There! We'll use that. If we can move it."

"We can move it!" Daisy said firmly. "We have to."

It took a while. Although the drawers were only half-full, they had to remove them, setting them aside while they made another try at hefting the huge piece up over the edge of the faded oriental carpet. It kept getting stuck, and they were both sweating profusely by the time they had moved it only a few inches.

Working together on the same side of the dresser, they lifted one side and swung it sideways, and then did the same to the other side. A slow process, but it did the trick. They continued until the dresser was flat against the stairwell door. Then they reinserted the drawers.

Exhausted, they sank down on the neatly made bed.

"You think he won't be able to move it?" Daisy asked, staring at the dresser.

"I hope not."

"Of course," Daisy looked over her shoulder uneasily, "we don't even know that he's *up* there."

Molloy's head turned slowly. "What?"

"Well, we don't. Just because he took Lynne up to the attic doesn't mean he's still upstairs. He came down here to nail the windows shut, didn't he? We don't know that he ever went back up. I mean, he could be down *here* now, somewhere. Or in the cellar. We don't know, do we? Maybe all we've done is made sure he stays down here with us. We barred the door, so unless he can move that huge dresser, he can't get back upstairs. If he used the main staircase, we'd see him or hear him."

Molloy thought about that, the expression on her face one of hopeless despair. Then it cleared, and she sat up straighter. "Okay," she whispered, "so maybe he *is* down here. Somewhere. At least we know he's not up in the attic with Toni. If he was, we'd have heard something. Toni would have screamed or pounded on the floor or something. She probably put something in front of the door up there, just like we did here. But," Molloy stood up, "we have to get back up there. So we have to decide which one of us is going for help. How do we decide that?"

But Daisy bent just then to pluck a clean, dry pair of socks from the bedside table, and let out a soft sound of delight. "Look! Look, Molloy, it's a radio! If the batteries are good, we can at least find out if the highway is open. If it isn't, whoever leaves will have to go back down through the woods and take that back road.

"Try it!" she urged, "but keep the volume low."

The strains of music were faint, but audible. "Oh, it works!" Molloy cried softly. "Get a news station, Daisy, anything in the area."

Daisy spun the dial, her ear close to the small brown box.

They heard the voice at the same time. The strong, deep tones of an announcer.

"Turn it up!" Molloy leaned closer to Daisy. "Is he talking about the weather?"

"This is WKSM news," the voice said, *"with an update on the tragic murder earlier this evening of noted psychology professor, Dr. Milton Leo, at his office on Faculty Row on campus."*

Daisy and Molloy, holding the radio up high between them, locked eyes. Murder?

"Police have notified the administration and nearby communities that the killer is still at large."

Molloy gasped. Killer? At large?

"They have, however, assured administration officials and surrounding communities that they do have a list of suspects, who are being questioned at this time. Meanwhile, they have urged citizens to remain on the alert. Doors and windows should be locked at all times and residents are advised to remain in their homes. Police say the inclement weather has been an advantage, since the roads, which are still flooded at this time, have remained clear of vehicles that the fugitive might confis-

cate for his flight from justice. Law enforcement officials are convinced that impassable roads have kept Dr. Leo's attacker in the area, possibly taking refuge in an abandoned or deserted building to wait out the storm. Stay tuned to WKSM for additional details on this developing story."

Daisy switched off the radio with shaking hands. *"Killer?"* she whispered. *"Killer?"*

"It's not him," Molloy said breathlessly, struggling for control of her emotions. "It can't be, it's not him. It's just some homeless person, like we said, who panicked when he saw Lynne. Probably thought she'd have him arrested for being here, remember?" Barely restrained panic filled her voice. "That's what we *said*, Daisy! Isn't it? *Isn't* it?"

"That guy on the radio said an abandoned or deserted house, Molloy. This house is deserted, isn't it? At least, it was before we got here." Daisy bent automatically to pull on the clean, dry socks, as if she didn't even know that she was doing it. Her fingers shook. "He must have got here before us, and now he's furious that we intruded on his hideaway. That's what's going on, Molloy, and you know it as well as I do. Anyway," she straightened up and looked Molloy full in the face, "didn't we already know he was a killer? Lynne isn't dead, thank God, but that's no thanks to him. He hit her and he left her for dead."

"We didn't know he'd already *killed* someone else," Molloy said, her voice shaking. "We didn't know he was a fugitive."

"Well, now we do," Daisy said angrily. But her voice wasn't any steadier than Molloy's.

They sat on the bed for long moments in a terrified silence, their eyes glued to the heavy, old dresser propped against the door to keep a killer away from them.

Chapter 16

Ernie finally managed to convince the two po-
licemen that he hadn't been anywhere near the
Leo house on Faculty Row when the doctor
was killed and that although he wasn't a fan of
the psychologist, he hadn't hated him. His
roommate, reached by telephone, affirmed his
alibi, saying that yes, Ernie was at his word
processor writing when the attack took place.

With an alibi and no apparent motive, de-
taining Ernie Dodd any longer would have been
a waste of time.

"Okay, you can go," Officer Sloane said.

Ernie hesitated. "What I want to know is,
while we've been wasting all this time, has anyone bothered to check out Nightmare Hall?"

Sloane frowned. "Say again?"

"I meant Nightingale Hall. It's an off-campus
dorm down the road. Gloomy old place? Top of
the hill overlooking the highway? You guys

been there yet? There's no one there right now, and the guy on the radio said the killer would probably be looking for a deserted place to hide in until the roads clear. Nightmare Hall sounds perfect to me. Has anyone been there to look for your guy?"

Neither officer knew. "I think they're still searching the dorms," Reardon said, "but I'll check." He left the room, returning a few minutes later to say, "Nope. No one's gone off-campus yet. Chief says with the main highway flooded, the fugitive is probably still hanging around here."

"Maybe he is," Ernie said, "but maybe he's *not*. Look, I've got friends out there in that storm. They might be stranded out there somewhere by high water, and I don't like the idea that *he* could be out there, too, okay?"

"I think he may have a point," Reardon told his partner. "I know the house. Been called out there once or twice. And at six-thirty tonight, when the crime took place, the roads weren't that bad. The murderer could have made it that far. Might have holed up there, especially if it's empty."

"It *is* empty," Ernie insisted. "And it'll only take us a few minutes to check it out."

Sloane's bushy, graying eyebrows lifted. "Us? No 'us' here, son. We don't take civilians along on police business. Tell you what, though. I have to stay here to finish up our interrogations, but Reardon here, if he can get through, can go take a quick look if the chief says it's okay."

"He already okayed it," the young officer said, nodding. "I told him what Dodd said, and he agreed that it was a possibility. And I'll get through. I'll take the back road." To Ernie, he said, "I'll drop you at your dorm. And I'll let you know," he added kindly.

It was clear that Ernie wasn't being given a choice. No way were they going to let him go along.

Okay, so he'd let Reardon drive him to the dorm.

But he had no intention of staying there.

In the attic at Nightingale Hall, Toni fought down the nausea that was threatening to overwhelm her. It had been growing steadily since Daisy and Molloy left. Toni attributed it to the shock of finding Lynne with her head caved in, and to the fear that clung icily to her bones, and to the stale air in the dark, still room at the top of the house.

She needed some air.

She had been crouched on the floor beside the trunk afraid to move, for a long while, one of her hands holding one of Lynne's, her other hand gripping Arturo as if she expected someone to rip him from her at any second. When she tried to get up, she found that her legs had fallen asleep, and had to stomp her feet repeatedly to get the circulation flowing again. Thankful that she wasn't wearing shoes, which would have made stomping noisy enough to be dangerous, she walked on still-tingling feet as far as she could toward the window. When the low-hanging rafters made walking impossible, she sank to her hands and knees and crawled the rest of the way.

When she reached the window, she had to kneel to tug at the sash.

The window refused to open. She couldn't see well in the darkness, but she could feel the latch, and knew it wasn't locked. She tried repeatedly, throwing her entire body strength into the effort to open the window, but it was useless. She gave up, sinking back on her heels.

She had to have air. If she didn't, she was going to pass out, and what good would she be to Lynne then?

Returning to the trunk, Toni checked Lynne again. Still looking as if she were sleeping, still unmoving, but . . . still breathing.

It wouldn't hurt to leave her for just a few, tiny minutes. Maybe there was a window on one of the other floors that would open. If she could just drink in a few gulps of fresh air, even if she got wet in the process, she could come back up here and keep her vigil until Molloy and Daisy brought help.

Toni didn't consider herself a brave person. She knew that going down those stairs, leaving her safe refuge, was dangerous. Hadn't she been the one to warn Daisy against venturing out of the attic? A sudden feeling of isolation swept over her as she realized that she had no way of knowing what was going on down there.

Were the phones working? Or had Daisy or Molloy been forced to leave the house to seek help? They had promised they wouldn't both leave her. Where was *he* now? Downstairs? Upstairs? Second floor, third floor, first floor, cellar?

She couldn't know.

What she did know was, she needed to get some air soon, or she was going to pass out, fall to the floor in a heap, and be of no use to anyone.

She *had* to be of use to someone. Staying up here with Lynne wasn't much, but it was something.

Tucking the bedspread more firmly underneath a waxen-faced Lynne's chin, and clutching Arturo tightly, Toni made her way through the obstacle course of old furniture, boxes, and trunks to the stairway. She was annoyed to find that her body was trembling. She took a deep breath, tiptoed down the stairs, and cautiously opened the door into the third floor hallway.

At the bottom of the hill behind Nightmare Hall, on the back road, Officer Reardon's headlights illuminated a silver Toyota Camry, its nose submerged in a ditch full of running water. He stopped the police car in the middle of the road and, leaving his lights on, went to investigate.

On the first floor, Daisy and Molloy left the bedroom to go back into the kitchen, sweeping it with the flashlight to make sure it was empty. Then they hurried to the wall of windows over the sink, intent on smashing a window to create an exit.

The third floor hallway seemed quiet to Toni as she pushed the attic door open very slowly, one inch at a time.

All she needed was one window . . . just one, and just for a few minutes. Then she'd rush right back upstairs, maybe even barricade the door with an old trunk or piece of furniture until she heard Daisy or Molloy's voice telling her it was okay now.

The air on the third floor was cooler than in the attic. It felt wonderful. Toni took several deep breaths. Her nausea begin to ease. As long as she was down here, it would be nice to find a bathroom. She could wet a cloth, soak it, and take it back upstairs with her. That would help. Lynne could use one, too.

There was a bathroom on the third floor, but it was completely empty. No washcloths, no towels, not so much as a piece of paper to soak with water.

The desire for a cool, wet cloth had grown so strong in Toni she couldn't give up on the idea now. And as she made her way along the darkened hallways and stairs, and nothing jumped out at her from a doorway, she became braver and more determined.

The second floor was only a few more steps down. There would be a bathroom there. If it had even one remaining paper towel, she could use that. Tear it in half, soak it, give Lynne one half and keep one half for herself.

Convinced now that she couldn't face the hot, airless attic again without that cool, damp cloth, Toni felt her way down the stairs slowly, carefully, quietly, to the second floor. A pang of guilt assailed her as she felt along the walls for a bathroom door. If Molloy or Daisy should come along, they'd be annoyed that she'd left Lynne. She'd have some explaining to do.

But she had been very quiet. They probably hadn't even heard her come downstairs. And she certainly wasn't about to call down to them. *He* might hear, wherever he was.

Toni peered through the darkness. Where *was* he? It was so quiet up here, the only sounds her shallow, rapid breathing and the rat-tat-tat of the storm outside. If he were up here, wouldn't there be some way to tell? Some sound, some *feeling* that she wasn't alone?

She felt alone. More alone than she ever had. At least when she went out on stage, she shared it with a pianist.

Still, she had Arturo. She was never really alone when the violin was in her hands.

She began hunting for a bathroom.

When he had turned off his headlights, Officer Reardon used his flashlight to search for footprints in the mud along the wildly rushing ditch. The prints he found had pooled with water now, but were still visible. The water was so high he had to move downstream and cross by walking on a fallen tree. Then he backtracked and followed the puddled footprints up the hill.

Ernie Dodd was on his way to Nightmare Hall when a security guard stopped him and wanted to know what he was doing "running around campus" at this time of night when there was a killer on the loose. It was shortly after midnight.

"Looking for someone," Ernie answered, his voice sharp. All he wanted to do was find Molloy. Why did people keep getting in his way?

The security guard wasn't giving up so easily. He insisted that Ernie get in his car while he tried to reach Officer Sloane to verify Ernie's statement that he'd already been questioned and released by the police.

Officer Sloane wasn't that easy to reach. Fuming, Ernie slouched in the back seat of the security guard's car, wondering if Officer Reardon had reached Nightmare Hall yet. And what he'd found when he got there.

In the kitchen at Nightingale Hall, Molloy heaved a chair at the widest window over the sink. The glass shattered with a satisfying sound. She and Daisy moved to the counter to pick the jagged glass remnants free of the frame.

The door that Toni opened first wasn't a bathroom. She knew that the minute she entered. The shadowy bulks that rose out of the darkness weren't fixtures, they were furniture: two single beds, a desk and chair, a low, squat dresser with a mirror that reflected the rivulets of water streaking the long, narrow window straight ahead of her.

A window!

Toni went for it like a homing pigeon zeroing in on its destination.

She yanked up the sash. There was no screen in place. The white lace curtains danced around her as the wind and rain accepted her invitation to enter the house. She drank in the cool, damp air like someone drinking water after a desert trek.

Officer Reardon was having difficulty tracking the footprints. He thought about returning to the car to call for assistance, but decided to forge on ahead instead. Plenty of time to call for backup when he got to the top of the hill.

Toni's face, her faded print dress, her hair, were wet in seconds, but she didn't care. She stood with her back to the room, her face raised to the sky. And she began to feel so refreshed, so revitalized, that she stood at the window longer than she had intended to, holding the violin case behind her back to protect it from the elements.

She was so lost in the pleasure of breathing air that when the violin was snatched from her hands, it took her several seconds to realize what had happened. She had heard no footsteps, no sound of a door opening further, no creaking boards behind her.

But suddenly her hands were empty. Arturo was gone.

Instead of fear, rage swept over Toni, and she whirled in a fury, prepared to do battle for her most precious possession.

She never got the chance.

The violin case was tossed to the floor.

Hands reached out and pushed, hard.

Toni stumbled. Her hands flailed out, clutching for the lace curtains, for something, anything, to keep her from sailing out the open window.

The wind picked up the lace curtains and cruelly whisked them out of her reach.

The hands pushed again, harder this time.

Without a sound beyond a terrified, breathless gasp, Toni flew backward out the window.

She was halfway to the ground before she screamed.

Chapter 17

Molloy and Daisy, at the kitchen window picking shards of glass from the white, wooden frame, heard the scream.

In one terrifying moment, their heads shot up, their eyes met briefly then flew to the darkness beyond the window. They watched in horror as a dark figure fell to the ground and lay motionless in a narrow puddle of muddy water, the arms and legs splayed out around it.

Daisy grabbed the flashlight, shone it through the window. "Oh, my God, it's Toni!" Daisy said in a choked voice. "If she fell all the way from the attic . . . !" She would have jumped then, through the open window, if Molloy hadn't grabbed her arm and, speechlessly, pointed to several large, jagged shards of glass still protruding from the white window frame.

Looking heartsick, Daisy's eyes went back to Toni.

Paralyzed with shock, the two sat on the counter, unable to think, speak, or move. Then one of Toni's hands moved. Only slightly. But it meant that she was alive.

Hope stirred Molloy to act. "The mud must have cushioned her fall," she said. "She's still alive. Let's get this glass out of here and then we'll go get her."

There was no response from Daisy, who sat beside the window staring at Toni.

"Daisy," Molloy pressed, "she's *alive*! Come on, help me with this glass. Hurry!"

They worked on the remaining slices of glass together, but several were embedded in the frame so tightly, Daisy finally had to deliver a blow from the flashlight, smashing the stubborn chunks to pieces.

Then they had those pieces to contend with. Daisy cut her hand in a half dozen places, brushing and pushing them aside. Ignoring the cuts, she grabbed the flashlight, plunged through the hole and jumped to the ground. Molloy was right behind her.

"Over here!" Daisy shouted and dived into the thick curtain of rain. "She's over here!"

But when she reached that spot and found

nothing but mud, she turned and said, "No, I think she landed over this way a little," and moved in that direction. There was nothing there, either.

Daisy did this three times, moving sideways in opposite directions, then in a circle, sending the flashlight in an arc that encompassed everything around her.

Toni wasn't there.

They *had* seen her fall, seen her land, seen her lying motionless in a little river of muddy water.

But she was no longer there.

When they looked up, they saw the open window and the white lace curtains blowing wildly in the wind. Toni hadn't fallen from the attic, after all. She'd fallen from the second story.

But that wasn't much consolation now that she was missing.

Toni's scream as she plummeted had reached Officer Jonah Reardon in the woods. A sinking feeling that he was already too late swept over him, and he struggled to speed up his uphill climb. He knew that scream should have sent him back down to the car. He should call for back-up before going into Nightingale Hall. But that would take forever, and there was that scream. He would have to wait to make the call.

Cursing the mud that sent him slipping and sliding sideways, he struggled up the hill, over its crest, and onto Nightingale Hall's sloping back lawn.

The house was dark, but he could hear voices to the right of the house, and ran in that direction, one hand on his flashlight, aimed in front of him, the other on his gun. When he rounded a corner of the house, he saw two people in what struck him as bizarre clothing, their hair and clothes drenched, waving a flashlight around and screaming someone's name. Their voices were frantic. The name sounded like "Tony."

When they saw him, they began to scream.

"It's okay, it's okay!" he said quickly, hurrying forward. "Police. Officer Jonah Reardon. What's going on here? Do you live here?"

"It's Toni," the taller girl in the black skirt and white blouse said anxiously, "our friend. She . . . she was up there . . ." pointing up to an open window on the second floor, "and she fell. We *saw* her fall, but when we got out here, she was gone."

The other girl, blonde, wearing a coat, shook her head and said, "She couldn't be gone, she couldn't! We saw her fall! She was up in the attic with Lynne, but she fell from that second-story window up there." She pointed. "She couldn't possibly have got up and walked away. Couldn't have. . . . Besides, she *didn't fall*, he *pushed* her, I know he did, only we don't know where he is, and . . ."

They were both talking, shouting, so fast, and making so little sense, that Reardon knew his first job was to calm them down. He suddenly felt totally out of his depth. He hadn't been on the force that long, these girls weren't much younger than he was, and he had almost no experience in calming down hysterical, terrified people.

"Let's just go inside, okay?" he said. "You can tell me all about it in the house. Here, I'll get the door."

"We can't go in that way. It's locked."

"Locked? You stopped to lock the door after you saw your friend fall?"

"No!" Daisy pointed toward the window. "We broke the glass and jumped out through there. We were locked in. The windows are nailed shut and the doors are locked, the keys gone. To get back inside, we have to crawl in through that hole we made."

Reardon knew he could force the back door open. But if Dr. Leo's killer was here and he'd tampered with the door, the door was now evidence. Better leave it alone.

They overturned a metal pail and used it as a step to crawl back in through the window.

When the two girls allowed themselves to realize that a police officer was there, they were able to calm down somewhat and explain everything that had happened. Except where Toni was. *That*, they couldn't explain.

"You're sure you saw her fall?" he asked patiently when they had finished their tale. "I mean, from what you've told me, you have every reason to be pretty upset. Scared out of your wits, actually. Sometimes fear does funny things to our senses."

"You mean our minds," Daisy retorted sharply. "There's nothing wrong with our minds, Officer, or our eyes. We saw Toni fall, and we heard her scream."

Remembering the scream that he had heard, Reardon nodded. "I should go back to the car and call for help. When I make that call, we'll have reinforcements here in seconds. Are your phones still out?"

Daisy nodded. "At least, they were. I'll check again. But you come with me, both of you."

The phones were still out.

Reardon wrestled with his choices. "My car's down there next to yours on the back road. But I don't want to leave you two alone while I go back down there." He paused, then added, "I guess I could take you with me."

"I'm not leaving Lynne," Molloy said, shaking with cold now that her clothes were saturated again. "And Toni, wherever she is."

"Me, either. Besides," Daisy added, "going all the way back down there would take you forever. You have to do something *now*! Find Toni. Find whoever hurt Lynne."

Making up his mind, the officer moved toward the hallway. "Look, you both stay right here, okay? I'll just take a quick look around, check on your friend in the attic, see how she is, so I'll know what to tell the paramedics when I call them. Then I'll go back to the car and make that call."

Chief will chew me out for coming in here without back-up, Reardon told himself. But he didn't see what choice he had. He couldn't leave these girls here alone, and they were in such bad shape, they'd slow him down considerably on his trek back down the hill to the car. If the girl in the attic trunk was in as much trouble as they'd said, time was critical here.

Officer Jonah Reardon had seen with his own eyes what someone, who must have been very, very angry, had done to Dr. Milton Leo's skull.

I guess I'm not as brave as I thought I was, he told himself wryly when he noticed his gun hand shaking as he moved up the first few stairs toward the second floor.

When he got to the second floor, he went to the open window and yanked it shut, locking it, knowing he was probably messing up a decent set of fingerprints. But he had a feeling there were plenty of other prints around this huge old place.

He found nothing on the second floor beyond various sizes of muddy footprints that he assumed belonged to the girls. The third floor was equally empty, and his stomach churned uneasily as he opened the door to the attic stairs. If the guy was still in the house, and he hadn't been on the first, second or third floors, how many floors did that leave? Only one. The attic.

He could be down in the cellar, he thought, as he opened the attic door.

The girl in the trunk looked bad, but she was breathing. Whether she lived or died, it seemed to him as he stood at the trunk feeling her weak, thready pulse, depended upon how soon he could make that call and get an ambulance out here. Would they even be able to get through? They'd better, he thought grimly, or we're going to have another death on our hands.

She moved then, one wrist, and only slightly, and made a sound that was half-groan, half-whisper.

If she awoke and saw the gun in his hand, she would be terrified. Laying it down on the bedspread covering her, he bent over the girl. What had they said her name was? Linda? Lynne, that was it. "Lynne?" he asked, checking her pulse again. "Lynne, can you hear me?"

He did hear the creak of a board behind him, it wasn't as if he didn't hear it, and he straightened up and reached for the gun, just like he'd been trained to do, but the bedspread was slippery, and so was the gun.

It slid out of his reach. It slipped and it slid on the old, faded chenille bedspread and then it was gone, disappearing into the dark depths of the trunk, and there was no time to dig down deep for it and pull it out. No time, because something made a whooshing sound behind his right ear and then something very, very hard hit the side of his head and his body flew to the right, crashing into a dress form and knocking it to the floor before he collapsed on top of it. A jagged piece of metal from the broken form drove itself into his chest as he landed.

Just before his eyes shut, Jonah Reardon saw again Dr. Milton Leo's crushed skull and thought, I should have been a teacher, Ma, like you wanted. Too late now.

Too late . . .

Chapter 18

Molloy and Daisy, waiting for Officer Reardon in the first floor entry hall at the bottom of the stairs, heard the crash from above when he went down.

"What was that?" Daisy breathed. Molloy gasped and clutched the dark wooden stair railing.

"It might not mean anything," she whispered in desperation. "Maybe he tripped over some of the stuff in the attic. It was so cluttered up there."

"He had a flashlight," Daisy said, beginning to back away from the stairs, her eyes on the second story landing. "He would have been able to see where he was going." Her gaze went to Molloy's face. "That killer is up there, Molloy, don't pretend he isn't. We wanted to know where he was, and now we know. Try the phone again. Hurry!"

Molloy fumbled for the phone, picked it up. Nothing. "No," was all she said.

"Okay, I'm out of here," Daisy said, and whirled toward the hallway.

"What?" Molloy ran after Daisy, already making her way down the hall toward the kitchen. "Where are you going?"

"Reardon said he parked his car down by ours. I'm going down there. It has to have a police radio. If I can figure out how to use it, I can call for help."

"Daisy, at least wait and see if he comes back down. It was probably nothing. I don't want you going out there by yourself." They reached the kitchen, and Daisy strode purposefully toward the broken window. "And I don't want to stay *here* by myself."

"I know, Molloy. I don't like it, either." At the sink, Daisy turned to face Molloy. "But we really don't have a lot of options here. That cop is down, and we both know it."

Molloy knew she was right. The windows and doors were barred against them for a reason.

"We felt safer with a cop in the house," Daisy continued, "but now that he can't help us, we have to do this ourselves. And I don't know any other way than getting down to that car.

If I can't make the radio work, I can drive for help."

She climbed up on the counter. "The thing is, we only have one flashlight. I have to take it, Molloy. I'd never make my way through those woods without it. I'm sorry."

"No, it's okay. I can see fine." A lie, but at least she knew her way around the house pretty well now.

"I'll be back as soon as I can. Find some place to hide and stay there until I get back. Remember," Daisy added as she slid her legs through the windowframe, "the back staircase is barred, so he can't come down that way. You could hide in the library and keep an eye on the front staircase."

And if he does come down, then what? Molloy wondered, shivering with fear and an overwhelming feeling of abandonment as Daisy jumped to the ground and ran off into the storm. What do I do if he shows up at the foot of the stairs?

She could only pray that the killer didn't have Officer Reardon's gun.

Molloy's legs were so weak, she had to lean against the kitchen sink. Her eyes kept going from the cellar door to the housemother's bedroom door, to the kitchen archway. He was here. Inside the house. He could come through any one of those doors at any time. He had murdered that psychologist, tried to kill Lynne, thrown Toni from a second-story window, and done who knows what to Officer Reardon.

Tears of frustration stung her eyelids. If he hadn't attacked Lynne, she told herself in fury, we would have left this house without ever knowing he was here. We couldn't have told anyone where he was hiding, because we wouldn't have known.

Then she remembered the noise they'd heard from upstairs, when they first arrived, and she knew that wasn't true. Ernie would have said, "Someone was murdered tonight and the police think the killer is hiding out somewhere around here until the roads clear." And then she and Lynne would have looked at each other, both thinking the same thing at the same time, and one of them would have said, "Nightingale Hall. He could be at Nightingale Hall. We heard a noise upstairs."

That's why he wasn't about to let them out of here alive. He knew they'd heard him. He knew they'd tell.

Four of them had come into this house. One of them was lying unconscious in a trunk in the attic. One of them had been pushed from a second-story window and was missing. One had left the house to seek help.

That left only one other witness to report that a fugitive was hiding in Nightmare Hall. Molloy Book.

A sound from upstairs sent Molloy flying out of the kitchen and down the hall into the library, where she crouched behind the overstuffed couch, her panicked eyes searching the darkness for a better place to hide. She didn't see one.

She hid there for what seemed like hours. She heard other sounds, faint scratching sounds and dull, distant thumpings, but she heard no footsteps on the front stairs leading from the upper floors down to the first floor. Telling herself the other noises could have been made by a squirrel or a mouse, wanting desperately to believe that, she wrapped her arms around her bent legs and huddled against the back of the couch, struggling to think through her fog of fear.

Daisy found the trek down the hill easier than climbing up it. She slid most of the way, as if she were sitting on a piece of cardboard on a snowy slope.

The creek was her biggest problem. The

water had risen several inches since they crossed it. Frothing and foaming like a mad dog, it churned through the woods like a raging river.

Daisy surveyed it with hopelessness in her eyes. On the other side, in the distance, she could see the police car, parked in the middle of the dirt road as if it had been waiting for her all this time. Had Reardon left the keys in the ignition? Probably not. But she could start it without a key. She knew how.

What she didn't know how to do was swim. And the body of water in front of her, which was probably a harmless little creek in good weather, looked like it would swallow her up the second she stepped into it.

Daisy walked a little way to her left, then to her right, hoping for an opening, a place where the water seemed shallower, tamer.

Her only hope was the huge boulder that had nearly flattened them into mulch. It was lying peacefully now, in the middle of the creek, looming up out of the darkness like a large, gray hippopotamus seeking respite from the heat.

If she could get to that boulder . . .

With the aid of the flashlight, she located a long, thick tree branch lying on the ground. She picked it up, clutching it tightly.

Okay, here goes nothing, she told herself, taking a tentative step into the water, then another. If it hadn't been for the tree branch, which she had implanted firmly in the bed of the creek, the swirling waters would have knocked her off balance instantly. The water rose to her hips, and its force took her breath away.

With the aid of the branch, which she repeatedly thrust into the creek bed just ahead of her, maintaining her grip on it, and then half-walking, half-floating forward until she was alongside it, she made her way to the boulder and clung to its rough, sharp edges, fighting to catch her breath. The rushing water tugged at her. Daisy held on, thinking of Lynne and Toni and Molloy.

The car, the car, I have to get to that car, she told herself over and over, and by doing so, managed to pull herself up, an inch at a time, to the top of the boulder. She lay there, wet and cold and shaking violently, until she had enough energy to stand upright.

The flashlight was gone, lost to the turbulent water. But she was halfway there, halfway across the creek, halfway to the police car and its radio that would make everything all right again.

Rain pouring down upon her, Daisy looked

down at the raging creek and thought, I can do this. I can.

Steadfastly refusing to think of what would happen to her if she failed, Daisy Rivers gathered all of her remaining strength together and jumped from the boulder, aiming her body toward the opposite bank of the creek.

Despite her exhaustion, despite the extra weight added by sodden clothes, the slender figure, arms outstretched for balance, legs kicking for momentum, seemed almost graceful as it flew through the air above the churning water and landed, face-down, on the muddy bank.

Only Daisy's feet and legs still belonged to the creek. The rest of her was safely on solid ground.

Not taking the time to rejoice, she pulled her legs free and stumbled up the bank to the police car.

The doors were unlocked. Daisy, almost collapsing with exhaustion, yanked the blue-and-white door open and slid into the front seat, pulling the door closed after her.

It felt incredibly wonderful to be out of the rain and the wind. She wanted nothing more than to lay her head back against the seat, close her eyes, and breathe deeply until she felt restored again.

But there was no time.

The radio was at hand, beside her right arm. It looked simple enough. She was pretty sure that all she had to do was take the receiver from its console and say something into it, anything, until someone answered her.

It's almost over, she thought, reaching for the receiver. Relief washed over her as the creek water had. I'll get the police, send them to the house, they'll find Toni, and the paramedics will fix up Lynne and that young police officer, good as new.

She picked up the small, smooth, black mouthpiece and began speaking into it, saying whatever came into her head. "This is Daisy Rivers, I'm on the back road behind that place called Nightingale Hall and there's a killer in the house and my friends are hurt. Someone, someone answer me, we need help, answer me!"

Not a sound came from the console. It was as silent as the telephone had been.

Daisy turned the receiver over in her hand. Fumbled at the console with her other hand, feeling for a switch, a knob . . .

Just as her fingers touched the wires protruding crazily from the bottom of the console, wires which she knew with sickening certainty should have been attached to something, a voice in her ear said, "Even if it was still working, which it isn't, you'd have to push in the button, stupid," and strong, angry hands came from behind and fastened themselves around her throat, squeezing until small black and red dots danced before Daisy's eyes and she could no longer breathe.

I made it this far for nothing, was her last thought before she slid into a void that was as dark and deep as any wild and raging creek.

Chapter 19

In the security guard's car on campus, the guard finally reached Officer Sloane and was told that Ernie Dodd had been checked out and was free to go. Then the guard explained to a thoroughly frustrated Ernie why they couldn't go looking for Molloy and her friends.

"Not my job," the guard said staunchly. "Campus and campus personnel only, that's my territory. Your friends, they're not students here."

"Well, they *will* be, if they ever get here!" Ernie cried. "They're already preregistered for the math session. Doesn't that count?"

"Not as far as I know," the guard insisted stubbornly. "They don't become my responsibility until they show up on campus. Sorry, fella, but with everything that's going on around here tonight, I wouldn't dare leave, anyway. Got a murder on our hands, y'know."

"Would I be this worried if I *didn't* know? Okay, then, if you won't help me look, at least use your radio to find out if Officer Reardon found anything at Nightm . . . Nightingale Hall. He was on his way there after he dropped me off at my dorm. Call, okay?"

The guard made the call. Talked for a few minutes. Replaced his radio. "No one's talked to Reardon," he said. "I just talked to Officer Sloane. He said Reardon's probably still checking the house and grounds."

Ernie was aghast. "Reardon dropped me off a *long* time ago. He should have been back on campus by now if there wasn't anything there. Is Sloane sending someone else to see what's going on down there?"

"No reason to." The guard's voice was maddeningly calm. "Look, kid, like I said, we've got our hands full here. We're handling it. Relax, okay?"

"Relax?" Ernie threw the car door open. Rain assaulted him. "A killer's on the loose out there, my friends are missing, and what you're telling me is that you don't intend to do anything about it."

"Can't. Sorry. Doing my part right here on campus. You need town police, maybe the state police. Might try calling them."

"I can't," Ernie bit off angrily, "the phones

141

are out. Thanks for nothing." He got out of the car, slamming the door much harder than necessary.

Tanner Leo's words kept ringing in his ears as he slopped through puddles. "If I were going to look for a fugitive, I know where I'd look. Nightmare Hall."

No one had heard from Reardon?

That seemed almost as dire as no word from Molloy. At least with Molloy, he could blame no word from her on the state of the phones. But Reardon had his radio.

Why hadn't he used it by now?

Maybe . . . maybe he couldn't.

The possibility of Reardon, a trained police officer, discovering something at the off-campus dorm that he'd been unable to deal with, turned Ernie's steps in the direction of his dorm. He *was* going to Nightmare Hall. Someone had to. But he wasn't going empty-handed. He'd find something in his room . . . a hammer, one of his weights, anything, to use as protection.

Simon and Elise were waiting for him, sitting on the floor outside his room, playing cards. Arthur Banks was with them. All three looked like drowned rats.

"I thought you guys would be long gone,"

Ernie said, unlocking the door to let them in. "When'd you get here, Arthur?"

"He just got here," Elise said, getting up. "So did we. Simon and I ate, and then came back up here to wait for you. We finally gave up. I went to bed and Simon went up to Arthur's room to see if he could camp out there."

"I wasn't there," Arthur filled in as they all trooped into Ernie's room. "I was downstairs in the computer room until the electricity started acting weird. It's still on, but it's very shaky. Wouldn't be surprised if everything went black all of a sudden."

"We wanted to know about Molloy," Elise said as Ernie quickly changed into dry clothes and scanned the room looking for something to use as a weapon. "I guess you didn't find her yet. Where have you been all this time?"

"With the cops." He could use one of his weights, maybe. They packed a wallop. "They seemed to think I might have been the one who decimated Dr. Leo's skull."

"I can't believe the cops thought it was you, Ernie," Elise said. "Everyone knows you wouldn't hurt a fly."

"Everyone but the cops," Ernie said, hefting the weight. Seemed about right. Could he actually hit someone with it if he had to? Elise was right about him. But if someone was threatening Molloy, well, that was different.

"So I guess they didn't find that guy yet?" Simon asked.

"Guess not. It's my bet they're not looking in the right place. I think he's at Nightmare Hall."

All three stared at him.

"Nightmare Hall?" Simon shook his head. "What makes you think that?"

"It's isolated; it's off-campus. He wouldn't want to hang around campus, not after what he did . . . and Tanner Leo said it's empty now. The perfect hideout, if you ask me. A police officer went to check the place out, and he hasn't come back yet. Or radioed in. I'm going down there."

"You talked to Tanner Leo?" Arthur said, sounding astonished. "Tonight?"

"I had to. I know it's not the best time, but I had to know if she had any idea who killed her father and where he might have gone."

"Did she?" Simon's voice didn't register disapproval as Arthur's had. "Does she know who did it?"

"No. But she's the one who suggested Nightmare Hall. I would have been there by now if I didn't look like the criminal type. It's the long hair, I guess."

"So, were the police questioning Tanner?" Arthur asked. "I mean, she and her father weren't exactly the best of friends, from what I hear. And who says it had to be a guy who killed him?"

"We already had that discussion, Arthur," Elise said, getting to her feet. "We all agree it could have been female. But it wasn't Tanner. Tanner Leo wouldn't hurt anyone, not even her jerk of a father. She's not like that." To Ernie, she said, "We're coming to Nightmare Hall with you. If the killer is there, you can't go in there alone. That's nuts."

"Oh, right." Ernie glared at her. "Let's get a bunch of people together and go trooping up the driveway in plain sight. Then, we'd certainly catch him by surprise, wouldn't we?"

Elise looked hurt.

"Sorry," Ernie amended quickly. "Look, there's something else I'd rather have you do. There's this cop on campus, Officer Sloane. Middle-aged, balding, bushy eyebrows. He was at the infirmary, but he's probably left there by now. See if you can find him. If you do, tell him I lied about my alibi, and got my roommate to lie, too. Tell him you know I did it."

Elise looked at him with a blank expression on her face. "Did what?"

"Killed Dr. Leo," Ernie answered impatiently.

"Ernie!" Arthur, his mouth full of chocolate-covered raisins, swallowed. "You want us to lie to the cops?"

"You have to. Tell them I've gone to Nightmare Hall. Because . . . because I heard the housemother hid money in the house, and I needed money to get away. Or make something up, I don't care. Just get the cops down there, and fast!"

"This is not a good idea, Ernie," Simon said, his eyes on the weight in Ernie's hand. "Gotta be a better way."

"There isn't. And I've wasted too much time already. Maybe Molloy isn't in that house. Maybe she isn't anywhere near it. It's not like I have any reason to believe that she is. But she *could* be, and I'm pretty sure *he* is. There's only one way to find out for sure."

"Well, you're not going without me." Simon went to the door, leaned against it. "Elise and Arthur can go find Officer Sloane. Me, I'm tagging along. Won't do me any good to be pitching like a champ if I'm missing my second baseman."

Ernie knew Simon meant it. The truth was, he was grateful. Reardon had gone to Nightmare Hall alone, and no one had heard from him since. It *would* be dumb to go into that place alone.

"Do you really think you can get through?" Elise asked as they all left the room. "I mean, the radio announcer said that the highway was closed between campus and town. That parts of it were flooded."

"Well," Simon joked, "we'll only walk on the parts that aren't flooded."

The last thing Elise said to them as they parted outside of Devereaux was, "We'll find Officer Sloane, Ernie. I promise. And we'll make him go down there. Good luck."

"We'll need it," Ernie muttered, and then he and Simon loped off across campus toward the highway.

Chapter 20

Three down, one to go.

It's so deliciously ironic that they tried to keep me from leaving. Me! Putting that dresser in front of the staircase door. As if that would stop me. A puny piece of furniture. What a joke.

It's only a few steps from that staircase to the cellar door leading to my outside exit. I've been going in and out the whole time, and they never knew it.

Hell, the cops aren't even close. Still checking the dorms. That'll take them forever. Lucky for me.

Even if my last little victim tried the cellar door, it wouldn't do her any good. I lock it from the inside whenever I go downstairs and, when I come back up, I lock it from the outside and pocket the key.

Meanwhile, I'm free to go wherever I want.

Unlike the little pigeon hiding in the library, with her wings clipped.

If she had half a brain, she'd have been long gone. Wouldn't leave her friends, though. How disgustingly loyal of her. I've never had friends who came anywhere close to that degree of loyalty. Wonder what it's like to have friends like that? Friends who don't turn on you, friends who wouldn't even think of deserting or betraying you. What is that like?

Dangerous; at least in her case. Very dangerous.

I wonder how long it will take all of them to figure out who killed Dr. Leo?

I'll be long gone by then.

Long gone.

But first . . .

Chapter 21

Molloy had no idea how long she crouched behind the couch waiting for Daisy to return. She had no sense of time. But after a while, the image of herself hunkered down in hiding made her stomach lurch in revulsion.

You're planning on putting yourself through college with no help from anyone? she asked herself in scorn. Where exactly are you going to get the courage for that, if this is the best you can do?

I'm the only one of us in this house who's still standing, she thought, getting to her feet. The folds of her long, wet skirt stuck to the carpet, and she had to tug on them. Lynne needs me. Toni needs me. And I'm not doing them any good curled up in here like a scared rabbit.

Daisy had done something. Daisy had gone for help. Until she returned, Molloy Book was the only hope for Lynne and Toni. A very scary thought. But true.

She had no flashlight. The house was very dark. She knew her way around a little, but she needed to see. Would there be a candle in the kitchen?

Her feet were freezing.

She would make her way to the kitchen, run into the bedroom and get a pair of socks, and then hunt for a candle and something to light it with. The stove, maybe. If it wasn't electric.

Where *was* he now? Upstairs? Downstairs? In the cellar? Her ears strained for the slightest sound. She heard nothing but the wind howling around the house outside, and the fainter sound of steady rain assaulting the windows.

In the kitchen, she had to fight against the overwhelming urge to climb through the broken window, as Daisy had. Molloy had never wanted anything as much as she wanted to leave that house, run as far away from it as she could, until she was totally, completely safe. Her eyes went to the back door. There was something so terrifying about knowing that she couldn't simply walk over to it and yank it open. That it was locked against her, making her a prisoner.

She went into the bedroom for a pair of socks.

And slammed, in the darkness, into something huge and solid. It knocked the breath out of her and she stumbled backward, almost falling. Catching herself in time, she felt with her hands to see what the thing was.

The dresser. The ugly old dresser that she and Daisy had struggled to move against the door to the back staircase, to barricade it.

What was it doing in the middle of the room?

Oh, *no*! He had moved it. Shoved it out of his way somehow, so he could enter the first floor.

Was he down here *now*? Where? In the closet? Under the bed? Behind a door somewhere?

Molloy listened again. Nothing. If he was down here, he was being very, very quiet. Hiding somewhere, quiet as a spider. A poisonous one.

Lynne had probably never even known what hit her. Someone must have come up behind her quietly, stealthily. Toni, too, probably hadn't sensed what was coming before she flew out that window.

That's *not* going to happen to me, Molloy thought with fresh resolve. She stood up very straight. She grabbed a dry pair of socks and sat on the bed to pull them on. Stood up again. Having warm, dry feet was amazingly comforting. *No* one, she thought again, is going to sneak up behind me. I'm not going to let that happen. I'm not sure how I'll keep it from happening, but I will.

What she wanted most was to run up the stairs to the attic and make sure Lynne was still breathing. And then race through the house opening every door in a search for Toni.

Some sense of self-preservation kept her from doing either of those things. She'd be making herself too available to him. She had to stay alive for Lynne and Toni's sake. And for her own, of course. The best way to do that seemed to be to stay in one place and defend it in every way she could think of.

For that, she needed light. And for light, she had to go into the kitchen. Where he might be hiding behind a door or under the table or in some dark corner.

She went slowly, lifting her feet without making a sound, feeling with her hands to avoid bumping into anything, her head constantly swivelling from side to side, her ears listening for the sound of breathing that wasn't her own. She heard and saw nothing.

Once inside the kitchen, she had to fumble through four kitchen drawers before she found two stubby white candles. She lit them from the stove burners, which were gas, after all, and set them on saucers from the cupboard. Her hands were shaking the whole time, her ears straining for the slightest noise from above or behind her, and every second she had to fight a strong urge to jump from the kitchen window into freedom. Only thoughts of Lynne and Toni kept her from doing so.

Besides, she told herself, seeking even the tiniest bit of comfort, he moved the dresser. Maybe he did that so he could leave the house. He could have seen the window they'd broken and climbed out through it. He could be long gone now.

When she had the candles lit, one stationed on the round wooden table at the far end of the kitchen, the other on the kitchen counter at her end, she felt better.

The candlelight allowed her to move about more freely. The all-white kitchen was long and narrow, the table and chairs at one end, the cabinets and appliances at the other, the floor worn linoleum. There were three interior doors in the room. Cautiously, carefully, Molloy checked out each of them. One opened into a pantry, sparsely stocked with a few cans and some paper goods. Another door housed an oversized washer and dryer, and Molloy guessed that the third wooden door had to lead to the cellar.

She walked over to it and tried the knob. Locked. Maybe it was always locked. Or maybe *he* had locked it, as he had all the other doors, and had the key on him.

That would explain a lot. If the cellar had an outside entrance, he could have been going in and out that way the whole time, using the back staircase. Even the heavy dresser hadn't stopped him.

He must be strong, Molloy thought, nausea rising in her as she turned away from the door.

A sudden image of Daisy climbing through the window and dropping to the ground appeared in Molloy's mind. That was quickly followed by the sight of the dresser moved away from the staircase.

Oh, no. Oh, no! Daisy? Had he gone after Daisy?

I went into the library, Molloy thought, her eyes widening in dread, and then I heard those scuffling noises, and now the dresser isn't barring the staircase. She leaned against the stove. Was that why Daisy hadn't come back yet? Hadn't she been gone an awfully long time?

Oh, he didn't, he didn't, she thought almost in prayer. Daisy was our only hope. He didn't follow her, chase her through the woods, catch her, and hurt her like he did Lynne and Toni. I won't believe that. I *can't!*

But if he had . . . if he had, then he knew that she was the only one left still standing in his way. With Daisy, and then Molloy, eliminated, he could stay in the house as long as he liked. Or at least until the roads were open again.

If he *had* gone after Daisy, had he come back to the house yet? If he hadn't, maybe she could keep him out. She could put something in front of the cellar door, in front of all the doors, and over the bare kitchen window, to keep him out.

Molloy laughed softly, bitterly. Get real, she told herself in disgust. How do you expect to do it by yourself? You couldn't lift anything heavy enough to keep him out.

She thought she heard something then, a soft, rustling sound from over her head. A tree branch brushing against a shutter outside?

How long would he wait before he came after her?

Why didn't he just *leave*?

But she knew he wouldn't. He was angry with them, with all of them, for disturbing his hideaway. If they stayed, he would have to leave his nice, safe refuge and go out into that awful storm, try to find another place to hide until he could leave town. That must have made him furious, or he wouldn't have done what he did to Lynne.

And now, he was punishing them. They were interlopers, intruders, and he couldn't forgive that. So he had trapped them inside this place and punished them, one by one.

She was the only one left.

How was she going to protect herself from him?

Molloy heard the sound again. This time, it seemed louder, not so much a rustling noise as a feeble scratching, like fingers on sandpaper. It wasn't coming from upstairs. It sounded very close . . . in this room somewhere.

There it was again, slightly louder this time.

Molloy took a few steps forward. The glow of the candle flickered across her face, turning it an eerie yellow. She was confused, uncertain.

Maybe it was him, trying to trick her. He'd draw her close to wherever he was, and then he'd lunge at her. She wouldn't stand a chance against the kind of strength it must have taken to move that dresser.

But the scratching noise grew louder, began to sound frantic. Molloy, her eyes on the far end of the kitchen where the noise seemed to be coming from, wished fervently that she had Lynne's baseball bat. She had to have something.

She grabbed a kitchen pot from the counter. It wasn't much but it would have to do.

The noise was coming from behind the louvered doors that hid the laundry equipment. That was a large enough closet to hide even a big person. Was he in there? Trying to trick her?

The pot, hard and solid though it was, suddenly seemed harmless and useless.

But Molloy walked slowly, quietly, over to the doors, her socked feet sliding on the cold tile.

She slid the door on the left side open a fraction of an inch at a time.

"*Help me,*" a voice whispered, so weakly that at first Molloy thought she'd imagined it. "*Someone help me, please.*"

The voice didn't sound masculine. And although the announcer on the portable radio hadn't said whether or not police knew the gender of the psychologist's killer she didn't know many girls who could have hefted that dresser alone.

So, when the voice came again, whispering, "*Please! please!,*" Molloy, hoisting the metal pot above her head, shoved open both louvered doors.

There was nothing there but a mop and a broom, shelves holding laundry supplies and baskets, and the white, oversized, washer and dryer.

But Molloy still heard the noise. Tapping. Tap, tap, tap. Weakly, but steadily. Tap, tap, tap. Like . . . like fingers on glass.

Molloy bent at the waist, her eyes focusing on the washing machine's glass front.

And screamed at the sight of hair, wet and straight, plastered to a face streaked with mud and blood, the eyes glassy with terror and desperation.

Molloy's legs gave, and she sank to the floor, her face now level with the face in front of her. In spite of the mud, in spite of the blood, in spite of the way the glass distorted the features, she knew that face well.

She had found Toni.

Chapter 22

Molloy roused herself from her shock enough to yank open the glass door of the front-loading washing machine.

"Can you move?" Molloy asked. "I want to get you out of there, but I'm afraid you might have some broken bones from the fall."

Toni opened swollen lips. "Out," was the most she could manage. "Out."

Molloy got her out.

She half-slid, half-pulled, Toni from the washer. She was careful, gentle, but still Toni's face twisted in pain, and she cried out twice.

"I can't believe you're alive," Molloy said in awe as Toni collapsed to the floor. "We saw you fall from the window. But by the time we got out there, you were gone. This is where he brought you?"

"No." The left side of Toni's face was badly swollen, her lips puffy. Talking was difficult for her. "Into cellar. Later, up here."

"You could have suffocated in there." Molloy checked for broken bones. The left wrist hung at an odd angle. Definitely broken. Her eyes scanned the kitchen for something to place under Toni's head. "I'm going to get you a pillow. Be right back."

Toni screamed. She clutched the edge of Molloy's long skirt. "Don't! Leave! No!"

"I'm sorry." Molloy turned, knelt beside her terrified friend. "I won't, I won't leave, it's okay, I'm right here."

But Toni was shaking violently, from shock and pain and cold. And terror. It was clear that the thought of being left alone in the kitchen scared her to death.

"You've got to be covered up," Molloy said. "I think you're in shock." Toni looked so small, lying there on the faded linoleum. Molloy thought about that for a second. Toni *was* small. And lightweight. "I'll carry you. We'll snatch one of those big, white cloths off the furniture, and a pillow off the couch, and then we'll come back here."

Toni shook her head, wincing in pain. "No."

"Yes," Molloy said firmly.

She picked up Toni, who weighed more than usual in her damp clothing, and staggered down the hall into the library, where she grabbed a large, white furniture drape and a pillow from the couch.

Molloy was listening, with every difficult step she took, for the sound of danger approaching.

But they made it back to the kitchen without incident.

If he was back inside the house, he was staying hidden.

She wondered if wherever he was, he was watching them. Was that possible? The thought made her skin crawl.

Once Toni was lying on the floor, snugly wrapped, her head on a worn print pillow, Molloy propped a wooden kitchen chair under the back door knob, another at the cellar door, talking all the while, reassuring Toni, who seemed to be drifting in and out of consciousness. "Daisy went for help," she said with false cheerfulness as she secured the back door, then the cellar door. "She should be back any minute now, so you just rest and I'll take care of everything, okay?" She didn't add that she feared the killer had followed Daisy out of the house.

It wasn't until Molloy turned away from the cellar door that, in the shadows drawn across the floor by the candlelight, she noticed the footprints.

Fresh, muddy footprints. Big ones. They led

. . . she looked, following the prints with her eyes . . . into the bedroom. And, although she didn't check, she knew they probably led up the back staircase.

Unless he was hiding, this very minute, in the bedroom.

Molloy stared down at the footprints. They hadn't been there when she tried the cellar door a little while ago.

She almost laughed, bitterly, aloud. She was too late with the chair propped under the doorknob. He'd already come back in.

When, she wanted to scream, *when* did you come back in? I've been right here, in the kitchen . . .

But she *had* left it, to carry Toni into the library.

Just for a few minutes, she argued angrily.

A few minutes would have been enough. Hadn't she already decided that he had keys to the doors? How long did it take to turn a key, open a door, and dart into the bedroom and up the back staircase? He could have glanced in through any of the windows, seen that the kitchen was empty, decided to make his move.

He was in the house again.

She could tell that he hadn't climbed in through their broken window. There were no muddy prints near the sink. He'd have been concerned about being caught in the act if he struggled in that way. Besides, she told herself, he's probably been going in and out through that cellar door the whole time.

She wasn't as stunned as she might have been. Hadn't she known he wasn't through in this house? She turned away from the cellar door, leaving the chair in place. Hadn't she known that he wouldn't leave without punishing her, too, for intruding on his hideout? For spoiling things for him?

If you thought anything different, she told herself, you're a fool.

He must have overheard Daisy saying she was leaving, and followed her. If he'd caught up with her, if he'd done something terrible to her. . . . Daisy had been their only hope. No one would be coming to Nightmare Hall to help now, and he knew that. He could take his time now.

But sooner or later, he would come after her. If she propped a chair in front of the back staircase door, he'd just come down the front staircase. And that one was too wide to barricade.

I am *not*, she thought, her teeth clenched, going to sit here and wait for him to show up.

While she rummaged through the drawers in search of something, anything, to use against him, she continued to talk soothingly to Toni, who made no response.

Ernie and Simon took the back road to Nightmare Hall, on foot. Ernie was afraid a car might get stranded in high water. "Besides," he added, "it's faster through the woods, on foot." Because Simon was with him, Ernie had left the weights behind. Two against one. Not bad odds, even if the "one" *was* a killer.

They emerged, soaking wet and muddy, a short distance from the two cars parked on the dirt road, one in the ditch, one in the middle of the road.

"Dammit, I knew it!" Ernie cried, breaking into a run. "That's Lynne's new car!"

While he ran for the Camry, Simon approached the police car.

"They're not here," Ernie called a moment later. He slammed the door shut. "They must have hiked out on foot." He glanced up the hill. "Isn't Nightmare Hall up there? They're up there. I know it. But Reardon must be, too. Why didn't he call in, say he'd found them? He knew how worried I was."

"Ernie," Simon called, "you'd better take a look at this."

Ernie hurried to the police car. Simon was sitting on the front seat, holding up a handful of loose wires. "No radio," he said heavily. "Someone yanked it out." He glanced up at Ernie. "Not a good sign, Ern."

Ernie struggled to collect his thoughts. He'd found out too many things at the same time, none of them good. Lynne's car was in the ditch. The four girls were gone. So was Reardon. "He probably followed them up the hill," Ernie said. "But . . ."

"But maybe somebody followed *him*? Is that what you're thinking? Someone ripped out his radio and then went after him?"

"Or was waiting for him up there, stopped him from finding Molloy and the others, and *then* came down and ripped out the wires. Either way, it's not good."

A moan from the back seat startled them. Simon jumped out of the car, his body tensed, his hands raised in defense. "What was that?"

Ernie moved to the back door, peered in through the window.

A girl lay on the floor of the back seat.

"It's Daisy! She's hurt." Ernie yanked the door open, crawled into the back seat. "Daisy? Daisy, wake up! Are you alright?" He lifted her up onto the seat, shook her gently, tugged on the wet sleeve of her coat. "Daisy?"

She opened her eyes, put her hands to her throat, rubbing gingerly. "Ernie? Is that you?"

Her voice was as hoarse as the croak of a frog. She sagged against him, tears beginning to flow freely. "I'm not dead? Ernie, I'm not dead! I thought . . ."

"No, you're not dead. Where's Molloy, Daisy? And Lynne and Toni?"

Still crying with shock and relief, Daisy waved a hand toward Nightmare Hall. "Up there." She shuddered. "It's a horrible, horrible place! And *he's* up there. He hit Lynnie over the head when she was getting wood. She's probably dead by now, because I didn't get help in time. And he pushed Toni out of a window and now we can't find her . . ."

"Whoa," Ernie said, trying to grasp what she was saying. "Take it easy. You're safe now." But when her words registered and he realized the meaning of them, he had to fight to maintain control of his emotions. Lynne and Toni were hurt and Daisy was down here? Molloy was in that house alone with a killer?

If he got his hands on the maniac who had done all of this. . . .

"Where's Reardon, Daisy? The cop. This is his car."

"What? Oh, the policeman. We don't know. He went upstairs, he wouldn't let us come with him, and we thought now we were okay because a policeman was there, but then there was this awful sound from upstairs somewhere, maybe the attic, and he never came back down." Daisy had been leaning against Ernie's chest. She raised her head and, still holding a hand to her throat said, "I pretended I was already dead. I went as limp as I could and it worked. He thought he'd finished me off. I guess I thought he had, too. Ernie," she clutched at his jacket with her free hand, "you *have* to *do* something! We heard about the murder on the radio. I'm sure it's him, I'm sure it is, and Molloy is up there all alone with him!"

"I'll go for help," Simon said abruptly. "On foot, since we don't have the keys to this thing. You go on up to the house, Ernie, see if you can find Molloy. But take it easy, okay? Don't be a hero. Just get her out of there and let the cops find that guy later."

"Oh, no," Daisy cried, bolting upright. "You're not leaving me here alone! He could come back."

"You don't have to go on foot," Ernie said, disentangling Daisy's hand from his jacket. "I know how to start the car. You can drive it to get help. If you can get through. Take Daisy with you."

He helped Daisy out of the back seat and into the front. Then he fumbled with wires until the engine chugged and roared. Simon got in,

Ernie got out. He stood watching as Simon drove off slowly toward town.

He'll never get through, Ernie thought despondently. The storm hasn't let up. The roads couldn't be clear yet. But maybe he can find a house with a working telephone.

Knowing the chances of that happening were slim, Ernie turned and started making his way up the hill.

In the kitchen, Molloy unearthed a piece of clothesline from the back of a shelf in the laundry area, and glanced down at Toni. Her eyes were closed. Was she asleep? Or unconscious?

Not bothering with one of the candles, she darted out of the kitchen, ran down the hall to the stairs, and knelt on the sixth step from the bottom. Using her hands as eyes, she tied one end of the clothesline around the bottom of one railing support and stretched the rope as taut as she could before tying the other end around an opposite support. Even if he had a light of some kind, he might not notice the rope stretched across the stair. He'd trip over it, and she'd hear the commotion when he fell.

If she only had the baseball bat. What had Lynne done with it? The last time Molloy remembered seeing it, hadn't they been in the library? Did she have time to hunt for it?

It could be anywhere, even up in the attic. And if Toni awoke and no one was there, she'd panic.

I could take the frying pan off the broken door window, she told herself, checking the rope one last time to make sure it was tight. Then, if I hear him fall, I can hit him with the pan before he has a chance to get up.

It was a terrible plan. He had shoved aside the dresser and his footprints were huge. He had to be bigger and stronger than she was.

Maybe she could think of something better. If she only had more time. Where *was* he? What was he doing? How much longer would he wait before coming after her? What would he do to Toni when Molloy was dead? Was Lynne still alive up there? What had he done to the policeman?

She had to get back to Toni. Molloy got up from the stairs and moved toward the kitchen, but when she passed the telephone table, she impulsively reached down and lifted the receiver one more time.

A hand came over her mouth, another came from behind to encircle her waist in an iron grip, and a husky voice said in her ear, "You're trespassing on my property, so you don't get to use the phone. You don't get to do anything. Except die."

170

Chapter 23

Ernie shouted aloud in fury when he came to the creek. It boiled furiously, covering twice the area he knew it usually did. He and Simon had come here to fish. The day they'd gone fishing, this creek had been a quiet, peaceful, silvery stream meandering tranquilly through the woods. Now, it looked like a wild river.

He and Simon had walked across it, using stepping stones to keep their feet dry.

Not tonight. Tonight, the only way Ernie Dodd was going to cross this treacherous body of water to reach Molloy was to swim it, and he was not the greatest swimmer.

Ernie remembered how his father was always singing those corny old love songs about swimming the deepest ocean, climbing the highest mountain, to get to the person you loved. Ernie liked the sound of his father's voice, but he was a little too cynical to think much of the lyrics.

Now, it struck him that maybe they weren't so stupid, after all. Because he *was* going to swim across this creek to reach Molloy. There was no other way. That was a *killer* up there with her, not just some annoying little creep.

Not wanting the extra weight of his baseball jacket, he stripped it off and threw it to the ground, then took off his mud-laden sneakers. They seemed, suddenly, to weigh a ton. He didn't want anything weighty dragging him under.

In just T-shirt and jeans, Ernie Dodd took a deep breath, said a hasty prayer, and jumped into the swollen waters of the creek behind Nightmare Hall.

And he tried. With Molloy on his mind every single second, saying her name with every single, valiant stroke, he tried.

But it was hopeless. The creek that he had known as tame and a great fishing spot was gone, replaced temporarily by this raging, bubbling cauldron. From the moment he jumped in, he felt powerless against its surging current.

When he realized that swimming, especially swimming as poorly as he was, was futile, he began grabbing for rocks, for sticks, for anything that would keep him afloat, maybe even help him to the opposite bank.

All in vain. Every time he clutched at something, its wet slickness slid right out of his grasp.

Oh, Molloy, he thought, and wasn't ashamed at all that tough old Ernie Dodd had tears of despair in his eyes as the vicious current, caring nothing about how much Ernie Dodd loved Molloy Book, swept him downstream.

Chapter 24

Molloy gasped as the arm went around her neck, squeezing painfully. Her free hand dug into flesh, but since she bit her nails, they were harmless, and the grip didn't lessen. She kicked backward with one foot. It connected, with what felt like a leg in jeans, but the blow was as useless as her fingernails had been.

"The last captive," the voice behind her whispered. "I can take my time with you. There's no hurry, since your little messenger pigeon never got very far from the coop. You girls really shouldn't have trespassed, you know. It's not polite."

"*You* did!" she gasped. "*You* trespassed!"

The grip tightened angrily. "You really are stupid. You talk to me like that when I'm in the catbird seat here? You should be begging for mercy. *He* would have, but I never gave him the chance."

The darkness in the hall ahead of her began to waver like drunken shadows. Her head felt like it was about to explode. Toni was lying out on the kitchen floor, helpless. He would move from Molloy, when he had finished with her, to Toni, pick her off as easily as he might flick a fly off his arm. She couldn't let that happen.

She was still holding the telephone in her right hand. It was a black desk model, old and heavy, with a rotary dial. In order to dial in the dark, she had picked up the entire phone, not just the receiver.

"I *hate* you!" she gasped, and her right arm came up and sideways with all of the strength she could muster to where she thought, hoped, prayed, his head had to be.

She couldn't see, but she could hear the telephone collide with bone. It hit hard. He shouted an oath, released his grip. She heard his feet staggering backward. She whirled, saw a shape in the darkness, stumbling dizzily, holding its hands to its head, muttering obscenities.

He is *a killer*, Molloy reminded herself. And darting two steps forward, she struck another blow.

He went down. She saw his body go limp, saw his head loll to one side as he landed.

She couldn't believe it. The person she had feared the most, this dangerous, maniacal killer, was lying unconscious on the carpet in front of her. He hadn't murdered her. She was still alive.

Gasping for breath, her legs feeling like mush, her entire system shocked to the core, Molloy dropped the phone and ran for the kitchen.

Toni was still quiet.

Molloy didn't know what to do next.

Leave? Get out of the house while he was harmless and couldn't stop them?

And go where? And how could she carry Toni *and* Lynne? He wouldn't be unconscious long. She hadn't hit him that hard. She couldn't run out to get help and make it back here before he woke up.

And she couldn't leave Toni and Lynne here with him. When he did wake up, he'd be insane with rage. He'd take it out on them.

Molloy raced back down the hall again, and over to the stairs to untie the clothesline from the stair rail. When she had it in her hands, she turned to stare at the dark shape lying on the old carpet a few feet away from her. She was terrified of going near him. He could be playing possum; waiting until she got close enough, only to reach up and grab her legs, pull her down, and choke the very life out of her.

She would have to take that chance. She couldn't leave him here, unfettered. The second he woke up, he'd be after her and Toni. And then he'd finish off Lynne. And he'd get away with it, with all of it. If she didn't stop him.

But she only had this one piece of rope. If she tied only his legs and left his hands free, he'd untie himself. If she tied only his hands, he could still walk or run to the kitchen and, although she couldn't see him clearly in the dark foyer, she could tell that he was big enough to harm her even with his hands tied.

The solution came to her then. She could use the clothesline to tie his hands to the stair railing. But first, she'd have to drag him over to the foot of the stairs. That wouldn't be easy.

Molloy had had many terrifying moments since she'd arrived at Nightmare Hall, but reaching out and grasping the feet of someone she knew to be a vicious killer proved to be her worst moment. She imagined him suddenly waking, the feet lashing out at her, kicking her in the midriff, sending her flying across the room. And then she would be helpless against his wrath.

Clenching her teeth so tightly that pain shot through her jaw, she bent down, grasped the feet, and pulled. He seemed to weigh a ton. His huge sneakers were covered with thick, gooey mud, and her hands kept slipping. But she held on, dragging the bulk one step at a time, until he was close enough to the railing that she could roll him over and wrap the clothesline tightly around his hands.

Then she tied the loose ends to the stair railing.

Now you're *my* captive, she thought with a wicked glee that startled her, almost frightening her.

"Molloy!" Toni screamed from the kitchen, and after hastily tying the last knot, Molloy picked up her skirt hem and raced down the hallway.

"I'm here, I'm here," she said, rushing to Toni's side. Her face looked worse than it had before, her bruises turning an ugly purple, her lower lip swollen to twice its normal size. Her head must have hit the ground hard. Without the mud, she was sure Toni's skull would have been fractured. This awful storm had its good side, after all.

"You can forget about him, Toni," she said, kneeling. "I smacked him a good one with the telephone, and tied him up to the stair railing. We'll be okay until help gets here. When that policeman who was here doesn't call in on his radio, they will send someone here to find out why, right? And we're okay until then. He can't hurt us now."

"Cold," Toni said, shivering under her white canvas wrap, "so cold . . ."

"What's wrong with me?" Molloy jumped to her feet, tripping on the hem of her skirt. "There's a teakettle and the stove is working, and I saw teabags in the pantry. Now that we don't have to worry about being attacked at any second, I'll make you some tea. But first I'm going to get rid of this skirt. It's driving me crazy. Time to shorten it." Reaching down, she ripped off the entire bottom half of the skirt. The fabric was old and flimsy, and tore easily. "There! Much better. I don't know how women got anything done in these clothes." Tossing the fabric aside, she filled the teakettle at the sink, put it on the stove to boil, her hands trembling the whole time, and went to the pantry to get teabags, keeping up a steady flow of pointless conversation in the hope that Toni would remain conscious. She felt less alone when Toni was awake.

Where were those police officers, anyway? Weren't they worried about their Officer Reardon?

"Listen," she went over to tell Toni, who seemed awake, although her eyes looked dull, "while the water's boiling, I want to go up and check on Lynnie, okay? I haven't been up there since we first came down, and I'm worried sick about her. Remember, I told you that guy is unconscious and tied up and he can't hurt you, right? So you'll be okay here while I run up the back stairs. I'll come right back down, I promise."

Toni nodded, but Molloy wasn't at all sure that she'd heard a word said to her.

Molloy didn't like the back staircase. It was fully enclosed, dark and shadowy, and very narrow. She had hastily grabbed one of the candles before she left the kitchen, but she had gone up no more than three stairs when a draught from above blew it out. It was almost gone, anyway. Now she was on the back staircase in the dark. But the prospect of turning around and going back down to use the front staircase was equally unpalatable. She would have to pass by her attacker, and she couldn't face that. She scooted up the stairs as quickly as she could.

Coming back down would be a different story. Maybe she could work up enough courage to go down the front staircase. Anyway, it was probably a good idea to check on him, make sure he was still out like a light.

She was breathing hard, and weak-kneed,

by the time she reached the top of the attic stairs, and realized that she was not only cold and exhausted, she was also very, very hungry. Nothing to eat since before they left at three yesterday afternoon. It had to be at least three or four in the morning by now. Twelve hours. She hadn't gone twelve hours without food since the last time she had the flu. No wonder she was weak. And she couldn't *afford* to be weak now. Not even a little bit.

"Lynne?" she said softly, hurriedly making her way through the boxes and trunks, bending low to avoid cracking her head on the rafters. "Lynnie, it's Molloy."

"Help me," someone groaned then from somewhere to the left of her. But it wasn't Lynne's voice. It was a man's voice, and it was full of pain.

For one shocked moment, Molloy thought the killer had escaped his bonds.

But when the voice came again, she knew who it was then, who it had to be. The policeman. Officer Reardon. This was why he had never come back downstairs.

At least he was alive.

Quicky glancing down at Lynne, still in the trunk, her breathing still shallow, Molloy called softly. "Where are you? I can't see you."

"Over here. On the floor."

Molloy felt her way to the left, pushing aside old lampshades and piles of magazines and moth-eaten sweaters and coats. "Keep talking, if you can," she instructed. "It helps."

"Can't . . . too hard. You're almost here, I can tell." Then he fell silent.

But she could hear his breathing. It sounded terrible, ragged and whistling.

She found him half-buried beneath a pile of old curtains that he must have pulled down on top of him when he fell. Tossing the curtains aside, she gasped in horror when she saw the skinny, tubular piece of black metal impaled in the center of his chest. Even in the dark, she could see the round, uneven stain of red encircling the tube.

"Let you down," he gasped. "Sorry. Came out of nowhere, the guy . . ."

"I know. Don't talk. I've tied him up, so it's okay. And I'm sure someone will be here any minute now. If they don't come soon, I'll have to go for help. I don't know what to do for you, though. You need a doctor."

"Cold," he said, echoing Toni's complaint. "I'm cold."

She covered him up again with the curtains, piling them high, and couldn't think of anything else that would help. Like Lynne, he needed medical attention.

She hated to leave him, and Lynne. But Toni was downstairs alone. Even with the killer tied up, she'd still be frightened. And she desperately needed something hot to warm her. The tea Molloy had promised.

"I'll bring you up something hot to drink," she told the injured officer. "And I'll see if I can find some bandages." But she knew she could never, not in a million years, pull that piece of tubing from his chest in order to bandage his wound. Hadn't she read somewhere that you should never remove an object that has penetrated the skin because the patient might bleed to death if you did? If she could just keep him warm, maybe that would be enough.

Then he lapsed into unconsciousness.

Molloy fought back tears as she made her way back down the attic stairs. She had no choices left.

She would have to go for help, as Daisy had.

But Daisy had never returned.

She would have, though, if the killer had been tied up when she left the house, the way he was tied up now. He couldn't have followed Daisy then.

And he wouldn't be able to follow Molloy now. Even if he regained consciousness, he'd still be tied to that railing.

Leaving the house was the only answer, she knew that. If the highway wasn't too flooded, she could run straight to campus and bring help back with her. If she couldn't use the highway, she'd have to take the back road. The thought of going back down that hill, through the dark, dreary woods, made her physically ill. But there might not be a choice. Making the decision was a relief, in a way. At least she had a plan now.

Toni would not want to be left alone.

Maybe, Molloy thought as she felt her way down the back staircase, intending to get a candle from the kitchen and check on her captive before she left the house, maybe I could carry Toni up to the attic. It's a long way, but Toni would feel much better if she were up there in that little room with Officer Reardon and Lynne. She'd feel safer.

It was worth trying. It would take up precious time, but Molloy knew she couldn't leave Toni lying, shivering, cold and terrified, on the kitchen floor.

The teakettle was whistling shrilly as she entered the kitchen. Toni was still quiet, huddled in her white swaddling. Molloy ran to the stove, lifted the kettle off the burner, and checked the one remaining candle. Nothing more than a fat stub, but it would have to do.

"Be right back," she said, "and then I'll fix your tea." Toni would have to drink it quickly. Then Molloy would take her upstairs, to the attic, before leaving the house. "I just have to check on something."

Holding the candle aloft, she hurried down the hall to the foyer.

She was only halfway to the stairs when she saw, in the dim, wavering glow of her little candle stub, that there was no one sitting on the floor of the foyer, arms tied to the railing behind him.

He was gone.

Chapter 25

She's going to pay.

How dare she? Tying me to the stairs like a dog.

She caught me off guard, that's all.

She should have done a better job with her knots.

I was only going to punish her for trespassing. But that wouldn't be nearly enough now. I'm going to take my time. It's not going to be quick and easy, like with the others.

It's her own fault. She brought this on herself. She has only herself to blame.

That's what he said. Dr. Leo said I only had myself to blame. But that's not true. It wasn't my fault. It was cruel of him to say that when it wasn't true.

It's true about her, though. She should have run screaming from this place when she had the chance.

Too late now . . .

Chapter 26

In Nightingale Hall's foyer, Molloy's feet halted in mid-stride, as if she'd suddenly hit a barricade.

He was gone!

The clothesline was gone, too. The glow of the candlelight revealed only the stairs.

She stood perfectly still, thinking for just a moment that she had imagined the whole thing: his arm around her neck, striking him with the telephone, tying him to the railing. Had she dreamed all of that?

No. It happened. She had left him unconscious, tied to the stair railing.

How long had he been free?

And where *was* he now? Molloy's terrified eyes quickly scanned the hall, but she saw nothing but dark, candle-softened shadows.

Toni! Alone, in the kitchen. He could have

gone upstairs and back down again by the back staircase.

Molloy whirled and raced back to the kitchen, so fast the breeze she created blew out the candle she was carrying. She kept going, anyway, feet flying along the faded carpet until she was on the linoleum again and at Toni's side. Her eyes quickly darted from one corner of the long, narrow room to another, looking for movement, a shadow, anything that would tell her they weren't alone. She saw nothing, heard nothing but the rain blowing in through the broken window and slapping into the sink.

Toni was conscious, but not alert. Her eyes were clouded, her mouth slack.

Anyway, it's *me* he wants, she thought, getting up. He's already punished Toni, and in the shape she's in, she's no threat to him.

She had to have a light. Darkness was too much of a disadvantage, especially if he had a flashlight. She needed to even the odds a little.

Moving quickly to the stove, Molloy lit all four of the gas burners. The flames did provide a minimal glow to the middle section of the kitchen.

What else could she do? There had to be something . . .

He must have removed his muddy shoes, or she would have seen footprints in the hall.

Tightening her lips in resolve, Molloy went to the kitchen cabinets to take out two tall, glass tumblers. With the glasses in hand, she hurried to the open archway between the hall and the kitchen and flung one of the glasses to the floor. It shattered, as she had known it would, into a pile of shards at the threshold. Let him step over *that* in nothing but socks. It might not stop him, but it should slow him down.

She took two more glasses into the bedroom, smashing one at the foot of the staircase, another in the doorway after she had backed out of the room.

She *had* to keep him away from her. She was the only one left to protect Lynne and Toni. The only one . . .

"Hey, there, what's all that racket out there in the kitchen? I can't have that. You're disturbing my peace and quiet."

The voice seemed to come out of nowhere, out of everywhere. Molloy felt as if it were all around her, like a cloud of toxic smoke, making her eyes water with tears of fright and her breath catch in her throat.

"You and your friends make lousy guests, you know that? You'd think you'd watch your manners, after intruding where you're not wanted. But oh, no, you just keep making noise and noise and more noise, and I CAN'T

STAND IT ANOTHER SECOND!" Shouting now, screaming, the voice coming closer and closer.

Molloy backed up to the stove. Her eyes never leaving the doorway, she reached behind her to grab the handle of the teakettle, still sitting on a lit burner.

And screamed in pain as the red-hot metal handle touched the flesh of her palm.

"Screaming already? But I haven't even touched a hair on your head yet. Or are you just practicing? Good idea. Nothing like being prepared."

Molloy bit her lower lip to keep from screaming again. She ran to the sink to run cold water on her burned hand, tears flowing freely down her cheeks now. I can't do this, she thought in terror and misery, I don't *want* to do this.

"You shouldn't have come here," the eerie, disembodied voice called. She thought it was coming from the hallway. He had heard her scream, and was headed straight for the kitchen. But she saw no light. If he didn't have a light, he wouldn't see the glass shards she had strewn in the doorway.

She could only hope and pray that he didn't have his shoes on. If he did, he'd just walk right over the glass. Wouldn't even slow him down.

"This isn't your place. It's mine. I would

have been fine if you hadn't showed up. Why didn't you just leave me alone? It's not my fault, what happened to your friends. And it's not my fault what's going to happen to you. You're to blame, all of you, for trespassing."

"*You* trespassed first!" Molloy shouted angrily. She spotted the bottom half of her skirt, a pile of discarded black fabric, lying below the stove. Ran over and picked it up, wrapped it around the burn on her right palm. Reached for the teakettle again, her hand protected by the wad of worn cloth, lifted the lid off the kettle and dropped it on the stove. She held the teakettle up, toward the doorway. Steam rose like smoke.

Molloy never took her eyes off the kitchen doorway. Her right arm, holding the teakettle high, shook violently, but she never eased her grip.

The voice had stopped, but she knew he was still coming. She could *feel* it. Any second now, she expected to see a dark form looming in the kitchen archway, or the sound of a cry of pain as he waded unwittingly into her pile of broken glass.

She was as ready as she could be.

Her eyes remained fixated on the doorway as if she were hypnotized.

But when she did hear a sound, it wasn't a

scream of pain, and it didn't come from the kitchen archway directly in front of her. It came from ten feet further down the kitchen wall, in the bedroom doorway. There was a clearing of the throat, and then, as Molloy's head swivelled in shock and her eyes flew to the source of the sound, the voice said with amusement, *"Expecting someone, are we?"*

Molloy shrank back against the stove. Bitter disappointment washed over her. The broken glass had been ineffective. Even with only the light from the burners, she could see the gray-white of his sneakers. He had put his shoes back on, after all.

Lynne's baseball bat was dangling from one hand.

"I'm not crazy like he said I was. Well, he didn't use that word, but he implied it. Wanted me to take the blame for my rotten life, when I had told him and told him that it wasn't my fault. He made that sound crazy."

"You mean that psychologist on campus," Molloy said. He looked enormous standing there in the doorway, almost filling it up. She couldn't see his face, and didn't want to. If she looked upon the face of a killer, she might never be able to forget it. "I know you're the one who killed him. But I don't see why you had to hurt my friends. What did you do to Daisy?"

"Who's Daisy?" His voice was lazy, uninterested. He stayed where he was, kicking idly with one sneakered foot at the slices and chunks and bits of glass that Molloy had placed there.

She knew he was playing with her. He believed that he had all the time in the world. And he probably believed, too, that she wasn't going to give him much of a fight.

Well, he was wrong. She had never been this terrified in her life, not ever. He was so much bigger than she was, and he'd already proved that it didn't trouble him at all to take a life. But he couldn't have hers. She wanted it. No matter how tough it got, how much it stank sometimes, how awful her parents were to Ernie, she still wanted her life. Because . . . because it was *hers*.

"How can I tell you what I did to this Daisy person if I don't know who she is?"

"You know who she is. You pushed one of my friends out of a window, and you attacked that police officer. And then you followed Daisy out of the house."

"Oh, that one. Choked her. Strangled her."

Molloy had to clutch the edge of the stove to remain upright. Oh, God, Daisy.

"Thought about tossing her into the creek. Man, you should see that thing now. It's a rag-

ing torrent! Had a real hard time getting back up here after that business with your Daisy-person. Could have killed her in the woods, but I had to get to the cop's car, anyway, to disable the radio." A laugh, crude and cruel. *"Killed two birds with one stone, you might say. Didn't throw her in the creek, though. Thought there might be a tiny chance that the cold water would revive her."* Another laugh. *"Didn't want that, I can tell you."*

While he was talking, he began playing with the baseball bat, hoisting it into the air, tossing it from one hand to the other, as if he were taunting her with it.

She knew what it would do to her skull, that bat. And it wouldn't bother him at all to do it.

She let him talk, her eyes circling the room. Back door. Locked. He had the key. No exit there. Then to the cellar door. Ditto. Then to the open window over the sink. The rain had stopped. There was no more windblown water spilling in through the hole she and Daisy had created.

Molloy fought the urge to laugh. The rain had stopped, the high water would go down quickly, the roads would clear, Ernie would be expecting her . . . but if the mad creature in the bedroom doorway had anything to say about it, Molloy Book wouldn't be continuing on to the campus of Salem University.

She had to stop his stupid, rambling conversation. Maybe he had all the time in the world, but Lynne and Toni didn't. Officer Reardon didn't. And maybe Molloy Book didn't either. She had to find out, one way or the other. She was ready. As ready as she'd ever be.

"I'm glad we came here," she said. "If we hadn't, no one would have known where you were. Now, you'll get caught. We'll tell." It sounded ridiculous even to her own ears, but she was hoping it would make him mad, stir him into action.

He threw his head back, laughing loudly. *"Oh, yeah, right, like any of you is going to be leaving this house. You're my captives, haven't you figured that out by now? You're not going anywhere."*

"I am," she said and, still holding the teakettle in her fabric-wrapped hand, turned and ran for the open window. He would have to run after her. That was what she wanted.

He was on her in seconds, yanking her shoulder, whirling her around to face him, shouting, *"You're not going anywhere!"*

"Neither are you!" Molloy shouted back, and

threw the contents of the teakettle in his face.

He screamed, staggered backward, cursing her.

And he dropped the bat.

Molloy bent, scooped it up, gripped it tightly, holding it over her shoulder as if she were about to receive a pitch.

Someone pounded on the back door. "Molloy! Molloy, are you in there?"

Without taking her eyes off the staggering, cursing figure, his hands to his face, Molloy shouted, "Ernie? Is that you?"

"Molloy, open the door!"

"Can't. Locked. Come to the open win . . ."

At the sound of yet another interloper, her attacker let out a bellow of rage and threw himself at her, his hands reaching out to encircle her throat. His beefy face was scalded red, his eyes tearing, the flesh on his lips already beginning to peel.

Molloy would never forget the sight of that face coming at her.

She couldn't hit him with the bat. Instead, she lowered it and hit him full force across his knees.

The blow stopped him just as his hands were about to fasten around her neck. He let out a scream. After a long, agonizing moment for Molloy when he stood right in front of her, hands still reaching for her, he sank to the floor and then toppled sideways, striking his left temple on the heavy metal handle of the dishwasher.

The sight of his eyes closing was the most wonderful sight Molloy had ever seen.

Weak with relief, she, too, sank to the floor, sagging against the white cabinets, trying to catch her breath.

A voice above her at the broken window called, "Molloy? Where are you?"

"I'm here, Ernie," she gasped, "I'm here."

Epilogue

They were gathered in Lynne's hospital room. Toni's room was down the hall, but she was sleeping peacefully. Daisy had already been released, and was sitting on the floor with her back against Molloy's chair.

"Dr. Leo should have known better than to suggest that Arthur go on a diet," Ernie said. He was standing behind Molloy's chair, his hands on her shoulders. "I remember once at Vinnie's, Elise asked Arthur if he really thought he needed that third burger, and he didn't speak to her for a week."

"He told me," Elise said from her station at the window, "that it was his mother's fault that he was heavy. That she used to make him sit at the table until he'd finished every bite of his dinner, and then she'd force dessert on him. He said she weighs about three hundred pounds and he thought she wanted him to look like her. 'Misery loves company,' was what Arthur said, and that's when I knew how miserable he really was, how much he hated being fat. But he never thought it was his own fault."

"I guess Leo told him it was," Simon said. He was sitting on the foot of Lynne's bed. "I should have guessed it was him when Ernie asked him to tell the cops that Ernie had done it and Arthur said, 'You want us to lie to the cops?' No one really knew who the killer was. It *could* have been Ernie. Sorry, Ern," grinning at Ernie. "The only reason Arthur knew for a fact that it would have been a lie was, Arthur himself had killed Dr. Leo. I just never picked up on it."

"None of us did," Elise said. "I knew Arthur had been out running around in the rain. He said he'd been in the computer room, but his clothes were soaked to the skin. He couldn't have got that wet just going from one building to another. But I didn't pick up on that, either, Simon. And then when we were supposed to be going to the police to tell them that Ernie had lied, he said he was feeling sick and could I help him up to his room? Like a fool, I did. Then he tossed me in the closet, locked it, and left. I had to scream my lungs out for hours before someone heard me over the noise of the storm and came to let me out."

"I still can't believe it was him," Ernie said. "Maybe we'd have guessed if we'd known that Arthur beat up a bunch of kids who called him Fatso a couple of years ago. Reardon told me that. The kids were only nine and ten years old, and Arthur really did a job on both of them. He almost went to jail, and had to undergo counselling for five years. That's why he was seeing Leo."

"He was sneaking in and out of Nightmare Hall," Molloy said. "Maybe not at first, but later that night, he had to. To follow Daisy, and then to come up to campus to talk to you. *We* were trapped inside, but he wasn't. He had those keys, and he knew about the cellar door."

"Well," Lynne said, "at least they've put him away now. Should have done it two years ago, and then none of this would ever have happened. Dr. Leo would still be alive, and we wouldn't have nightmares for the rest of our lives." She shook her head gloomily, then said crankily, "I just want to know how my new car is." Her head was swathed in white, but normal color had returned to her face. "Did anyone ever get it out of that stupid ditch?"

Ernie nodded. "We did, Simon and me. I'd rather have done almost anything than go back to where that nasty creek was, but I knew you'd throw a fit if we left your car there."

"I still don't understand," Molloy said, glancing over her shoulder at Ernie, "how you got out of that creek. You don't swim any better than I do, and I'm terrible."

"A log. I stopped in to see Reardon on my way up here. He's doing okay, by the way. Anyway, he said he walked across a log. Must be the one the creek slammed me up against. I just grabbed hold, that's all. Couldn't climb up on it, the current was too rough, so I overhanded it across. Couldn't believe it myself when I ended up on the opposite bank."

"When I first saw you, you looked like you hadn't made it across. A drowned rat, that's what you looked like," Molloy said, squeezing his hand. "But you looked pretty good to me, Ernie Dodd."

"The feeling's mutual."

They all fell silent then. Molloy knew they were thinking about Arthur. Officer Reardon had told them he often saw behaviors and attitudes similar to Arthur's in criminals. "They really believe that nothing bad that happens is their fault. That it's everyone else's. When Dr. Leo suggested that Arthur go on a diet, he was saying that Arthur was responsible for his obesity. Arthur couldn't handle that, and flew into a rage. What happened to him as a child really *wasn't* his responsibility. But what happened when he wasn't a child anymore, was. And he wasn't ready to face that."

"That place he's going to?" Molloy had asked the officer then. "Will they help Arthur handle all of that stuff? Will he ever be normal again?"

"That won't be their primary concern. Their primary concern will be keeping someone with Arthur's rage level and lack of conscience off the streets. But he'll probably be in there most of his life, so I guess they'll tackle some of those problems while he's there."

"Good news," Ernie told Molloy now. "The university has agreed to pick up the tab for all the damage to Nightmare Hall. They figure since it was one of their dorms, and you weren't safe there, you shouldn't be penalized for doing what you had to do."

Molloy liked the sound of that. Doing what she had to do. She had, hadn't she? It had been horrible, terrible, the worst thing . . .

But she had done what she had to do.

Couldn't be that hard to keep doing just that.

And *with* Ernie. Ernie, who couldn't swim worth a darn but had crossed a raging creek for Molloy Book.

Definitely with Ernie.

The pizza, which Lynne's doctor had expressly forbidden her to eat, arrived then. Simon locked the door when the delivery person had gone, and they ate.

Molloy grinned when Lynne selected the largest slice and devoured it with relish.

About the Author

"Writing tales of horror makes it hard to convince people that I'm a nice, gentle person," says **Diane Hoh.**

"So what's a nice woman like me doing scaring people?

"Discovering the fearful side of life: what makes the heart pound, the adrenaline flow, the breath catch in the throat. And hoping always that the reader is having a frightfully good time, too."

Diane Hoh grew up in Warren, Pennsylvania. Since then, she has lived in New York, Colorado, and North Carolina, before settling in Austin, Texas. "Reading and writing take up most of my life," says Hoh, "along with family, music, and gardening." Her other horror novels include *Funhouse, The Accident, The Invitation, The Fever*, and *The Train*.

Return to Nightmare Hall . . .
if you dare

Finished.
  Done.
  All of it down in black and white.
  Victims' names.
  Dates of execution.
  Methods of execution.
  All there. In a special code, of course. No one will ever figure it out. Even with the code, it could mean disaster if anyone else got their hands on the disk.
  And this, of course, is only for the first four victims. There will be more. Many more. If Phase I is a success, and why wouldn't it be, Phase II will follow.
  The mission now is to see the plan through, exactly as it's written down in the Death file.
  Time to Save the file. REDD, I've titled it. For REVENGE and DEAD. Revenge is my

goal, Dead is what they'll all be, each and every one of them. REDD.

Save file. There, that's done!

Close file. Done.

Exit file. Done.

Exit . . . I like that word. If all goes well, more than just the file will exit. Four people on this campus will exit as well. Forever.

They deserve to die for what they've done.

Can't be soon enough. Had to be patient for too long. But no more. It's time now.

Save.

Close.

Exit.

THRILLERS

High on a hill,
trapped in the shadows,
something inside a dark house
is waiting...and watching.

THE HOUSE ON CHERRY STREET

A three-book series
by Rodman Philbrick and Lynn Harnett

Terror has a new home—and the children
are the only ones who sense it—from the
blasts of icy air in the driveway, to the windows
that shut like guillotines. Can Jason and Sally
stop the evil that lives in the dark?

Book #1: THE HAUNTING
Book #2: THE HORROR
Book #3: THE FINAL NIGHTMARE

HCS1194